BAD BOYS

FRANK RODERUS

THORNDIKE
CHIVERS

This Large Print edition is published by Thorndike Press, Waterville, Maine, USA and by BBC Audiobooks Ltd, Bath, England.

Thorndike Press, a part of Gale, Cengage Learning.

Copyright © 2008 by Frank Roderus.

The moral right of the author has been asserted.

ALL RIGHTS RESERVED

The text of this Large Print edition is unabridged.

Other aspects of the book may vary from the original edition.

Set in 16 pt. Plantin.

Printed on permanent paper.

LIBRARY OF CONGRESS CATALOGING-IN-PUBLICATION DATA

Roderus, Frank, 1942–
  Bad boys / by Frank Roderus.
    p. cm. — (Thorndike Press large print western)
    ISBN-13: 978-1-4104-1132-7 (alk. paper)
    ISBN-10: 1-4104-1132-X (alk. paper)
    1. Large type books. I. Title.
PS3568.O346B33 2008
813'.54—dc22   2008035367

BRITISH LIBRARY CATALOGUING-IN-PUBLICATION DATA AVAILABLE

Published in 2008 in the U.S. by arrangement with The Berkley Publishing Group, a member of Penguin Group (USA) Inc.
Published in 2009 in the U.K. by arrangement with the author.

U.K. Hardcover: 978 1 408 42175 8 (Chivers Large Print)
U.K. Softcover: 978 1 408 42176 5 (Camden Large Print)

Printed in the United States of America
1 2 3 4 5 6 7 12 11 10 09 08

BAD BOYS

PROLOGUE

He stopped in the street outside the white-painted picket gate and stood there for a long, nervous moment before he let himself into the tiny yard. He followed a flagstone walk to the steps, then paused again for a deep breath before stepping up onto the porch. He removed his hat and spit in his palm, then rubbed his hand over his hair to slick down some of the spikes caused by the hat.

His palm tasted of salt sweat, another sign of nervousness, and of neat's-foot oil and boot polish. His stomach knotted and turned over in response to those combined flavors. Or perhaps for some other reason.

He could see his reflection in the etched glass in the front door. He did not find his own appearance impressive at the best of times and especially not today.

Licking dry lips and giving himself a stern reminder to breathe out as well as in, dammit, he tugged the bellpull.

And waited.

It seemed forever that he stood there on the porch. Waiting. Wishing he did not have to do this. Wishing he could just get on a horse and ride the hell away forever.

But there was more than just himself to be thought of here, and he wanted to be fair about this.

For just about the first time in his life he wanted to be fair and proper and above-board. About . . . everything.

Then he would leave. Or whatever. But he was not, absolutely was not, going to leave without explanation.

A dray went by on the street, the big hoofs of the draft horses raising small puffs of dust.

He turned, looked, adjusted the no longer familiar set of the pistol at his hip, licked his lips again.

Footsteps. Finally he could hear the approach of shoe heels on polished hardwood. He turned to face the door again and forced a smile onto his still dry lips.

The door opened and he reached up to snatch his hat off, only to remember halfway through the gesture that he was already holding the hat in his other hand. "G-good afternoon, Miz Hightower. Is Claire at home? I mean . . . may I speak with her? Please."

The woman smiled and stepped back. "Of course you may, Daniel. Wait in the parlor. I'll tell her you are here and fetch you children some lemonade."

"Thank you, ma'am. Thank you very much." He knew where the parlor was and which chair he should sit in and had even come to enjoy lemonade, particularly so since Clarence Hightower kept a sawdust-filled icehouse and served iced beverages in the worst heat of summer.

Daniel knew the way, all right. How many times had he been in this house? He could not begin to remember.

He wondered if he would ever be welcomed here again.

Claire's mother tap-tapped her way toward the back of the house at a dignified pace, and a moment later Dan heard the clatter of much quicker — and younger — footsteps racing up the back stairs. That would be the hired girl Yvonne being sent to inform Claire of the unexpected arrival of her . . . fiancé? Intended. The entire community knew, but no announcements had been made or banns posted. Her beau.

He heard more scurrying about upstairs and the rumble of Yvonne hurrying back downstairs. A few moments after that Yvonne came into the parlor with a tray bearing two stemmed water glasses and a crystal pitcher. She set the tray down and poured lemonade into both glasses, but did not serve them. Then she gathered up her skirts and withdrew into the kitchen end of the house.

Dan fingered his collar. It was choking him. And the hammer of the gun was poking him low in his side. It didn't used to do that, or anyway he did not remember it happening.

He heard light, measured steps coming down the curving front stairs and stood to greet the most beautiful girl who had ever graced the earth . . . or at least he so believed.

The sight of her fair took his breath away every time he saw her. This time was no different, except perhaps even more so.

"Miss Hightower." He nodded and very slightly bowed at the waist as she entered the stuffy, closed room. Lord, what he wouldn't give to open a few windows or something, but that would have allowed dust from the street to get onto the curtains.

"Mr. Southern." Her smile was glorious. Surely the reason the sun rose so faithfully each morning was so it could light Claire

Hightower's smiles. She crossed the room and stopped at her usual chair. "Please sit down. Would you share some lemonade?"

"Thank you." He sat. He felt a runnel of sweat trickle down the side of his neck, and the hammer of the damn gun was prodding him again.

The lemonade tasted good, tart and sweet at the same time. More importantly it gave him something to do with his hands.

"What a beautiful day this is," Claire observed, beginning the verbal dance that was required of them, at least until public announcements were made concerning the future.

Dan could not bear the thought of going through all that. Not today. "Claire, we have to talk. Right now. About something real serious."

"Oh!" Her eyes — hazel, very large and in the right light sometimes looking positively golden and sometimes green — widened. "I . . . Is everything all right? What's wrong, Dan? You act . . . Is there someone else? Is that what you've come to tell me today?"

"God, honey!" He never before in his life had called her "honey," and this time it slipped out so naturally that he did not even notice the lapse of manners. "I won't ever love anyone else but you, not my whole life

11

long. Never."

"Then what . . . ?"

"I have to . . . I have to tell you . . . something. It ain't . . . isn't, isn't pretty. It's about . . . Claire, I have to tell you who I really am. What I really am."

"You aren't Daniel?"

"Oh, I didn't mean it exactly that way. I haven't changed my name or anything. Not that it would've done any good if I had. But . . . my true name is Daniel Robert Southern, just as I've said all along. But . . . my family, my past . . ."

"You've said so little, Daniel, about either."

"That was deliberate. And with good cause. You see . . . Oh, God. Claire, you are gonna hate me when you know the truth. And that is tearing my heart right out of me. But I want you to know the truth. It's time that you do. Then I'll . . . I'll leave. If you want me to."

"You're scaring me, Daniel. What could be so terrible? Whatever could you have done . . ."

"I want you to know it all, Claire. I still want you for my wife. More than anything in the world I want that. But you have to know the whole truth about me. I expect you'll send me away then. But I pray that

12

you won't.

"I guess . . . I should start all the way back when . . . it started." He took a gulp of lemonade that he very nearly choked on. He began then.

1

Eastern Kansas 1871

"What're you gonna be when you grow up?"

"I'm going down the trail for to be a cowboy. An' I'll have my own horse an' I'll carry a big ol' gun an' I'll drink likker an' kiss ladies."

"You're a liar."

"Am not, Henry Read, an' if you call me that again I'll knock your block off."

"Won't neither."

"I will sure enough."

"You watch what you say, Danny South'ron."

"Make me."

"Boys!"

Both instantly settled. It would not do to get Miss Addison angry with them, lest they be kept after school, and if that happened they would both catch heck from their folks, Henry from his pop and Danny from his ma.

"Go inside now," the teacher ordered.

"The bell hain't rung yet," Danny protested.

"*Hasn't* rung."

"Yes'm." He had known that. Of course he had. But it was easier and somehow more satisfying to use "hain't."

"The bell has not rung," Miss Addison said, "but there is someone I want you to meet."

A brief thrill of worry ran down Danny's spine. Who . . . ? He hadn't been doing anything wrong the other day. He really hadn't. Just chucking rocks. A little. He hadn't broken anything. At least he didn't think that he had.

"We have a new boy in school. He is just your age, and I think you two rapscallions should meet him."

Rapscallion. Danny was not sure just exactly what one of those critters was, but Miss Addison didn't say it like it was anything really bad. Sometime he ought to go to the big ol' dictionary kept open on the stand at the back of the schoolroom and see if he could find out what a rapscallion was. That dictionary was big enough to hold every word that there ever was.

Danny and Henry trailed Miss Addison into the little schoolhouse — even though

16

the bell had not yet rung — to find a pair of strangers there. One was a grown-up in bib overalls, a crisply laundered shirt and a necktie. The other was a boy, tall and thin and dressed exactly like his dad, right down to the carefully knotted necktie that puffed out from under the wings of his collar. A collar and tie. For school. Who ever heard of such a thing?

The most striking thing about the kid, though, was his hair. He had fiery red hair and all the freckles a body could want.

Miss Addison said the kid was Danny's and Henry's age, which meant he was ten and he was far from growing into himself, but he looked wiry and tough.

Danny decided he didn't like the new boy. He was a smart aleck and a show-off and seemed to make much of himself, coming to school wearing a necktie and all.

Shoes too. The kid was wearing shoes, and it wasn't anything close to being cold outside. Who ever heard of wearing shoes when you didn't have to? Unless you were a show-off. No sir, Danny most definitely did not like this kid.

Then Miss Addison smoothed the icing onto that cake. She said, "Daniel Southern and Henry Read, I want you to say hello to our new pupil, Wilbur Clybourne."

"Wilbur?" Danny blurted. "What kind of a name is Wilbur?" Then he burst out laughing.

"All right, children, you may . . ." The word "go" was drowned in the thunder of seventeen pairs of feet hitting the floor, chairs scraping and barely contained squeals of relief as the pupils — all but the oldest of them anyway — exulted in their escape to freedom.

Danny glanced to his right, where the new kid was getting up and gathering his slate and the burlap sack he'd used to carry his lunch. The kid had hardly looked in his direction all day long, never mind that the three boys and pigtailed Jessica Jones constituted the entire third grade. At lunchtime and during recess the new kid had gone off to sit by himself instead of trying to fit in. He was scared, Danny figured. Danny mocked him right to his face, and he hadn't done a thing about it the whole day long. He was chicken, that's what it was. This Wilbur kid was plain old chicken.

The little kids ran screaming out into the sunshine, and the older kids brushed past as if they did not even notice the existence of Danny and Henry. Danny was dawdling, waiting for the new kid to start for home,

18

and if Danny was hanging back, then naturally Henry was too. Finally only the three
boys and Miss Addison were left in the
schoolroom. And that was no good. Danny
did not want to be singled out for the
teacher's attention. He knew better than
that. He hurriedly grabbed up the bag his
mother had made for him to carry his slate
and lunch and things.

"Let's go," he hissed out of the side of his
mouth.

"What's the matter, hey? First you wait
till everybody else is gone and now you're
in such a big ol' hurry."

"Hush up, Henry, and let's go before she
sets us to washing the blackboard or somethin'."

Henry sighed in mock exasperation. But
he picked up his book bag and followed
Danny outside.

The new kid finished fiddling around with
his things and hurried out behind them as
if to walk along with them.

"Where d'you think you're going . . ."
Danny hesitated for half a moment, then
added, "*Wil*-bur?"

Wilbur didn't say anything, just followed
along close behind them.

Danny turned around and walked backward. He began a singsong chant. "Wil-bur

is a scaredy cat; Wil-bur is a scaredy cat; Wil-bur is a . . ."

Wilbur scowled and balled his hands into fists. His face was flushed as red as a new bandana. He threw his burlap sack onto the ground and launched himself at Danny, fists flailing and teeth gritted.

Danny dropped his bag and braced himself.

Not all of the kid's punches landed, but some of them did, and those punches hit hard. The first one that connected with Danny's face numbed the entire left side of his head. After that they were not too bad. They landed hard, but he could hear them more than feel them.

The blows landed with a hollow, melon-like sound. They rocked Danny but did not sting him.

After a few of them, he could feel blood running over his chin and down his neck, and the stray thought came to him that his mother was going to be mad at him for messing up the clean shirt that was supposed to last him for the week until she had a chance to wash again.

That dang Wilbur was a scrapper.

Danny considered himself pretty tough too, though. He gave back as good as he got, fists flying and brow knotted in concentration as he hit and shoved and snarled.

He blacked the kid's left eye and cut his lip and planted a big old mouse on his cheek and twice knocked him down and still the kid kept coming, kept throwing those punches.

Danny tripped and went down himself, and the kid stepped backward to give him time to get up instead of moving in and hitting him while he was down or kicking him with those shoes he was wearing. The truth was that Danny was mad enough he might have kicked Wilbur the times he was on the ground except Danny wasn't wearing shoes and did not like the idea of busting a toe or something. The kid was fighting fair though. Danny had to admit that.

And Lordy, he sure could fight hard.

The kid stepped back and bent over at the waist, gulping for breath while Danny crawled slowly to his knees and then staggered to his feet.

"I guess I whupped your ass," Danny said.

"Reckon I whupped yours," the kid shot back at him.

Then Danny began to laugh and the kid did too, both of them doubled over and running blood and laughing like hyenas. Or anyway like everybody always said hyenas laughed, that being an expression Danny had heard his whole life long even though he had no idea what a hyena looked or sounded like.

Both of them went to laughing and grinning and feeling good about themselves.

"Call me Red," Wilbur said.

"I'm Danny. This is my pal Henry."

Red went to laughing some more, and Henry looked back and forth from Red to Danny like both of them were crazy. Then Henry shrugged and grinned, and the three of them picked up their things and walked back toward town together.

"You wanna go for a swim? We got a good place at the bend in the creek. It's where we go fishing, but you can swim there too."

"I can't swim."

"Ah, it ain't deep. You can stand up anyplace there. Anyhow we got to wash all this blood off us. Might as well have fun doing it."

"Yeah, that's all right with me."

"Come on then, Red." Danny broke into a run upstream along the little creek that ran between the schoolhouse and the town. Red followed close at his heels, and so did Henry, who was nearly always content to follow Danny's lead.

■ ■ ■ ■

The three boys sat on a patch of sweet grass close by the creek, all three of them naked, drying off after their swim. They could hear the faint chuckle of water flowing over rocks and the skitter of squirrels in the trees nearby. The day was warm, and a shaft of sunlight reached them through a gap in the trees. Summer still had a few days left to give.

"Hey, Red."

"Mm?"

"Mind if I ask you something?"

"Go ahead."

"It's about them bruises on you. How'd you get those?"

"What bruises're you talking about?"

"Jeez, Red, you got bruises all over your back an' butt an' up high on your legs."

"Yeah," Henry injected. "You're a real colorful guy, Red."

"I didn't know that." Red shrugged. "From my pap, I guess. He whales on me sometimes, but I didn't know it left bruises. Guess I never looked."

"You aren't sore?"

" 'Course I'm sore, but I don't hardly pay it no mind anymore."

"Why's he do that, Red?"

"Oh, he gets mad or drunk or like that, or I do something that pisses him off. Then he beats on me. He tries to get me to cry, but I won't. I don't never let him see me cry, damn him. Never have."

"You've never cried?"

"Once. When my mom died. I cried then, I did. But not when my damn pap thrashes me. What about you?"

"I've cried a time or two."

"Me too," Henry admitted.

"Well, not me. Except for that once." Red plucked a stem of grass and chewed on it, gazing overhead toward a puff of white cloud that was floating past.

"What does your pap do?"

"He's a carpenter. How about yours?"

"My pop is dead," Danny said. "It's just me and my ma. She's Old Mr. Lewis's housekeeper."

"Who's he?"

"He's the richest man in town. Owns practically everything around here."

"How about you, Henry?"

"My mom and dad are both still alive. He's a barber. Has his own shop too. Owns the building and everything."

"I wisht . . ." Red scowled and shook his head, chopping the words short. He stood up and brushed the grass and bits of leaf litter off his backside. "I don't know about you guys, but I'm dry enough."

"All right." The others stood too and reached for their clothing.

"We'll see you tomorrow, Red."

"Yeah. That's . . . that's all right then." Red stuffed his feet into his shoes and ran off toward town before Danny and Henry finished dressing.

"Here." Red pulled a bulky fold of brown paper from his pocket. The three boys were seated cross-legged beneath a tree at the edge of the school grounds.

"Whatcha got?" Henry asked.

"Take a look and see for yourself."

Henry accepted the packet and carefully unfolded it, moving cautiously, as if he expected something to jump out at him as soon as he got it open. Then he looked up and grinned. "Horehound drops. I love horehound drops."

"Take them. They're yours."

"Gee, thanks." Henry held the paper open in the palm of his hand and extended it to Danny for him to share the dark, sticky candies there. Danny took one and popped it into his mouth. Henry did the same, then very carefully refolded the paper and put it in his pocket.

"That's nice of you, Red."

"I always take care of my buddies. You know? Always."

"Thanks."

"Whatcha got for us today, Red?"

"Got some licorice for you, Henry."

"Aw, jeez. You know I don't like licorice."

"Sorry. Next time I'll see if I can get some peppermint."

Henry grinned. "Good. I like peppermint."

The bell rang, calling the pupils in from recess, and all three boys jumped to their feet. It did not do to be late and incur the wrath of Miss Addison.

"Do you know what I don't understand?" Henry mused.

"You gotta give us a better clue than that 'cause you don't understand much," Red returned.

Henry ignored the gibe and said, "I don't know why they call themselves Musketeers when they're always fighting with swords."

"And why are they called the *Three* Musketeers when there's four of them," Danny put in.

"I don't know about that stuff," Red said,

"but I like that 'one for all and all for one' stuff. That's kind of like us."

"One for all and all for one. Yeah," Henry agreed.

"That's right. Just like those old guys," Danny said.

Red lay back with his hands laced behind his head and a grass stem sticking upright from the corner of his mouth. "Can you two musketeers sneak out Saturday night just after dark?"

"Why?"

" 'Cause that's when Sallie Benson takes her bath, that's why?"

"How would you know that?"

" 'Cause I seen her last Saturday. The window shade wasn't pulled all the way down. I stood on a crate an' peeped in."

"You saw her *naked?*" Henry squeaked, barely able to breathe.

"Bare-ass buck naked," Red assured them with a grin.

"What, uh . . ."

"She's starting to get titties," Red said.

That made Danny squirm to relieve a sudden crowding in his drawers, but it was not news to him. Sallie was one year older and two grades ahead, and Danny had indeed noticed that Sallie's shirts no longer hung flat on her chest. She had curly hair and dimples, and she was the prettiest girl in the whole school. In the whole town. Heck, maybe in the whole of Kansas. "You really and truly, honest Injun, saw Sallie naked?"

"I said so, didn't I?" Red said.

"I never seen a girl naked," Henry complained. "I heard they got no dicks."

"They don't," Red confirmed. "They got . . ." He paused for a moment to think, then sat up and held his two cupped hands together facing inward, thumbs together. "They look kind of like this?"

"Like hands?"

"No, dummy. Like this here. On top. But down here, of course."

"I don't get it."

Red grunted and resumed lying stretched out flat on the ground. "Come with me Saturday night. I'll show you."

"Are you in, Danny?"

God! Sallie Benson. Naked. Danny's breathing was rapid, and he was so hard he was afraid he might bust before he could get home to the outhouse and take care of that. His voice cracked a little when he said, "I'm in."

Red closed his eyes and pretended to sleep. But he was grinning.

"Are you all right, son?" Danny's mother

reached forward and pressed the back of her hand against his cheek, then frowned and shook her head. "You don't have a fever."

"I'm all right, Mama. Really."

"You've hardly eaten a thing. That isn't like you. Please tell me what is wrong."

"Nothing. I promise."

"Aren't you hungry tonight? Don't you like . . . ?"

"Mama! Please. I'm fine. I'm just . . . in a hurry. I promised I'd meet the guys."

"After dark?"

"Yes, Mama. Red, he said he thought he could get us some firecrackers. Maybe even some Roman candles. You know how I like Roman candles."

"I don't know, dear. I don't know what sort of boy this Red is. I hate to say it, but I hear things. About Red."

"He's my friend."

"Yes, but . . ."

"Mama. I have to go." Danny grabbed a chicken thigh and a hunk of bread and stuffed them into a pocket on his overalls, then hurried out the kitchen door before his mother had time to protest.

He ran through the alleys, stomach aflutter, and ducked into the shadows at the back of the barbershop. Henry was already there, sitting on an upended keg. "Did you have any trouble getting out?"

"No."

"Me neither."

"Where's Red?"

"Here I am."

"I didn' hear you come up. What are you, some kinda Red Injun?"

"Where do you think I got my name? Sure I'm part Indian. But tell me. What do you want to do now? Flap your jaws or go see if it's Sallie's bath time?" Red waited a few seconds, then said, "Follow me, musketeers, but quiet. Be quiet as real Indians, hear?"

Moving with exaggerated caution, the three boys crept to the other end of the block and across a litter-strewn vacant lot to the Benson house. They gathered, heads close together, and Red whispered. "You see that light over there? That's the washroom off the kitchen. That's where they got their tub. Now what we are gonna do, we are gonna be as quiet as if we was dead. Just walk real easy now. And don't go to laughing or giggling or anything, you hear me?" He scowled directly at Henry.

"Ah, I ain't gonna say nothing."

"No, but you make noises sometimes. You shouldn't ought to do that. She might hear. And mind you don't lean too close to the window lest she be able to look out and see us looking in. Now . . . be quiet, both of youse. Real quiet." Red turned and silently led the way until all three boys were standing on tiptoe with their foreheads pressed against the glass and their eyes glued to a thin strip of light at the bottom where the window shade did not quite cover.

Danny peeped in and immediately became light-headed and woozy. His breathing quickened and his heart raced.

The Bensons's copper-lined slipper tub had deep side walls, and the lamp that lighted the bathing area was set on a stand close to the door, so everything in the tub was backlighted and in shadow when seen from the perspective of the window.

But Sallie was there, her skin shiny with water, her hair pinned high, her image fixed indelibly in Danny's memory.

Lordy, oh Lordy . . . Red had not lied.

"Can you guys get away for a campout?" Red asked. "I was thinking we could take some fish line and hooks, spend a couple nights out along the creek. You know. Somewhere we ain't none of us ever been before."

"This weekend?" Danny asked.

"Any weekend."

31

"Maybe."

"I don't know," Henry said. "I don't know as my folks would let me go off by myself like that."

"You wouldn't be by yourself, dummy."

"You know what I mean."

Danny grinned and said, "If they knew you was with Red, that'd be worse than being by yourself."

"That's the truth," Henry agreed.

"Hey! What is it with you guys? Am I that bad an influence on you?"

"Yeah, you are."

"Why d'you think we like you?"

"You don't hafta tell them that I'm coming."

"They'd know it anyway."

"All for one and one for all," Henry said. "Everybody in town knows the three of us run together. You see one of us, look around, you'll see the other two."

"Getting back to that camping trip, is everybody in?"

"Yeah."

"You know we are."

Red grinned. "Good. 'Cause I got plans."

"But, Mama, I *have* to go. I already told the guys. You don't want me to lie, do you?"

"Daniel, I will not have you lying out there

on the hard ground like that. You'll catch your death of cold."

"Oh, we won't be doing nothing like that. Red has a tent," Danny improvised. No one he knew or had ever known owned an actual tent.

"Where would that boy get a tent?"

Danny shrugged. "His pap brought it home from the war or something like that."

Danny's mom sniffed. "I didn't know Mr. Clybourne was ever in the war."

"I think he was. Maybe. Anyway, he's got a tent, an' we're gonna stay in the tent, so it's all right that I can go, right?"

The sniff was followed by a loud sigh to indicate how put-upon she was. But she did say, "All right, but . . ."

Danny did not bother to listen to the "but" part of her comment. The important thing was that he could go on the campout with the guys.

Red passed the quart-sized canning jar to his pals. The liquid in it was a red-tinged brown, and the fumes coming off it took their breath away when they tried to sniff it. The three boys were lying on the bare, cool grass a mile or so north of town. They had a fire and one blanket — Henry's — for the three of them, and they were filled with a sense of adventure.

"Gaw-ly," Henry whispered. "What is this stuff?"

Red shrugged. "I dunno exactly. Mr. Wannamacher keeps a big jug of it in his carriage shed." He snickered. "So's Miz Wannamacher won't find out. It ain't locked or anything so I brought us a little."

"Without asking?"

"Aw, he'll never know. He'll never miss this little bit. That's the thing you want t' watch out for, see. If you take just a little an' leave most, it's never missed. How do you think I come up with all the candy an' crackers an' stuff I bring for us guys? Same thing. I slip into the general store or people's sheds or whatever and swipe just a little bit of what I want." He smiled. "It's easy. Tell you what. Tomorrow night I'll show you how. In the meantime, have yourself a swallow o' that stuff and pass the jar. I got me a thirst on."

2

Eastern Kansas 1875

"That sonuvabitch," Red grumbled. The three fourteen-year-olds were sitting close around a campfire in a thicket south of town. It was a spot they had come to think of as their own, for no one else ever came there, no one other than the occasional hog or cow. There were no crops nearby and no stream to attract visitors.

"Which sonuvabitch d'you have in mind?" Danny asked.

"Wannamacher."

"Oh. That sonuvabitch. What did he do now?"

"He run out of booze, that's what he done now."

"What's he done," Henry asked, "gone temperance or something?"

"I dunno, but the damn crock was empty last night when I went to draw off a little for us."

"So what are you gonna do?"

"We can get some from Tambor's saloon."

"They keep the back door locked tight as Mrs. Diggs's prissy ass," Henry said.

"Yeah, but I got a plan. It's just that I'll need some help. Are you boys in?"

Danny grinned. "Aren't we always?"

"Does a dog have fleas?" Henry said.

"Does a chicken have lips?"

"No, but it has a pecker."

"Funny. Very funny."

"The point is, we're in with you, Red, just like you knew we would be. Was that crock really empty?"

"Yeah, dammit."

"Then what are we gonna drink tonight?"

"I brought a quart of buttermilk. We can pass that around."

"Somehow it don't seem like the same thing as old man Wannamacher's red-eye."

"So shut up and listen to my idea for swiping some keg whiskey from Tambor's place."

"Can we get some tobacco while we're there? I don't have nothing to put in my pipe."

"Stuff your joint in there, Henry. It might feel real good."

"Aw, have you seen the size of that little pipe of his? No way he could fill it even if he's got a hard-on."

"I'm trying to be serious now and you guys are assing around. Do you think we can find some tobacco too?"

"No, but maybe I can think of something. Just give me a minute to come up with a plan."

"What are you kids doing in here? You're too young to be drinking, and I don't care if you have money or not. I won't be responsible for anything like that."

"Oh, we aren't here to try and buy anything, Mr. Tambor. My mom wouldn't put up with that."

"Then what is it you want, Danny?" The heavyset saloon keeper seemed more relaxed and agreeable once he learned the two boys did not want to buy liquor from him.

"I was wondering how a man goes about starting his own business, sir," Danny said.

"And you?" Tambor cocked his head and squinted owlishly at Henry.

"Me? Oh, I don't want nothing. I'm just with him."

"All right then. So what is it you want to know, Daniel?"

"Like I said. I been wanting to know how a body goes into business."

"What sort of business do you have in mind?" Tambor smiled. "You aren't think-

37

ing of giving me any competition, are you?"

Danny laughed. "No, sir. If I was gonna do that, I'd ask Mr. Harris."

"Now, why in the world would you ask Mel Harris about business if you intended to open a new saloon here in town, Daniel?"

"Why, because of him doing the freight hauling, he'd be the one wanting to get my business bringing in kegs of beer and stuff, wouldn't he?"

"That's something I wouldn't have thought of, Daniel. I like it. It shows you really do have a head for business, and I hope you never do decide to open another saloon. Now I —"

"Excuse me, I hafta take a leak."

Tambor and Danny seemed barely to notice when Henry slipped away, but the saloon keeper looked up a moment later when Henry emerged from the storeroom with a sheepish look.

"Sorry," Henry mumbled.

"You have to go out and around through the alley to get to the outhouse," Tambor said.

"Yes, sir. Sorry." Henry left, disappearing around the side of the building while Tambor and Danny continued their discussion about getting started in business.

Ten minutes later Red and Henry were waiting behind the wagon park, where Danny joined them. "What the hell took you so long?"

Danny shrugged, then grinned. "It was kind of interesting, what all he was saying." He looked at Henry. "Did you get it done?"

"Sure."

"So the door is unlocked," Danny said.

"Unless Mr. Tambor sees that the latch is off and sets it again," Henry agreed.

"So when are you gonna go in?" Danny asked Red.

"This afternoon. I'll do it when things get busy an' noisy inside."

"And now we just wait?"

"That's right. Say, do you guys wanna dig some grubs and see can we catch us some fish?"

"Yeah, that sounds all right. C'mon."

In the past Danny and Henry had enjoyed the fruits of Red's petty thievery, but they had not participated in the thefts. Not directly participated anyway.

This was . . . different.

And it was, Danny discovered, exhilarating.

Sneaking inside Tambor's saloon. The heart-stopping horror of imminent discovery that could happen without a second's notice. The fear that stabbed deep inside his belly and brought his heart leaping into his throat with every creak of a hinge or tap of a footfall. The prickling at the nape of his neck with every shout of triumph or peal of laughter from the saloon floor just those few paces distant. Oh, it was all wildly exciting.

It made him feel . . . *alive.*

He was so frightened he was afraid he might pee himself and give his fears away to the others.

Yet there was something quite magically intoxicating about this sense of flirting with danger.

The boys, all three of them, slipped inside the back door that Henry had unlatched earlier. They tiptoed through the rows of kegs, searching in the dim storeroom with no lamp or candle to light their way.

"Psst!"

Danny nearly jumped out of his skin at the sound.

"Found one."

He wished to hell Red would not talk so much.

"Here."

Red lifted the top of a small, sawdust-filled crate. He extracted a quart-sized bottle — bonded whiskey — hesitated and then pulled out another. He handed the second bottle to Henry. Secured a third bottle and handed it to Danny. It was cold and hard and brittle, and Danny clutched it so hard he was afraid he might break the glass.

One for each of them. The good stuff.

"C'mon. Let's get outa here."

Giggling and snickering and so relieved to have gotten away with the theft that he felt faint, Danny followed Red out the back door and into the alley. Henry was just as close on Danny's heels.

Lordy, that was exciting!

Danny looked at Henry. Passed out with puke all over his shirt and the front of his britches. Henry's mama was sure to give him hell when he got home. He turned his head away from Henry and looked at Red, who was sitting beside him at their hangout in the woods. "Know what I think?"

"What's that, kid?"

"I'm thinking likker ain't all that it's cracked up to be. I mean . . . I'm woozy right now. Couldn't walk a straight line if your life depended on it. Mine maybe, but not yours. And all it gets me is that tomorrow I'll be sick as a dog."

"Now that interests me, Daniel."

"What? That I'm gonna be sick?"

"No. What you just said."

Danny's brow furrowed as he tried to remember what it was that just came out of his mouth. Apart from a little spittle, that is.

"Sick as a dog. How sick do dogs get anyhow? And who the hell cares?"

Danny shrugged. "It's just an expression, I guess."

"Sure, but it's stupid."

"Most regular expressions are. Think about them close sometime. They mostly sound dumb as posts."

Red laughed. "There's another one." He shook his head. "Sick as a dog. Dumb as a post." Then he grinned. "Saves thinking for ourselves though, don't it. You want any more of this likker?"

"No, I'm done."

"For tonight," Red said.

"No," Danny told him. "I mean I'm done. Period. I had enough of that shit." He stood up and brushed off the back of his britches. "Next time, man, we oughta steal something worthwhile. If we're gonna steal, that is."

"Funny you should mention that," Red said. "I already been thinking about something along those lines."

With another glance toward Henry passed out on the ground, Danny said, "Not until he wakes up, eh?"

Red replaced the cork in the mouth of their remaining bottle of rye and stashed it inside the hollow log where the three of them kept their few secrets.

They hunkered down behind a screen of empty beer barrels. It was late on Saturday night, later than Danny had ever stayed out before, at least not without getting permission first or telling his mother that he was staying over with someone.

Danny had that fluttery sensation in his belly again and the tingle of anticipation that set his nerves on edge and his senses so acutely aware of every click of a cricket or flutter of a bat's wings. He was frightened. Yet at the same time happy. Excited. Oh, this was better than liquor any day of the week.

"Hsst. There's one." Henry's whisper was so faint it could barely be heard.

Red shook his head. "Not him. He ain't blind yet."

The drunk passed by, unaware of the boys who were lurking in the shadows. The man stumbled on about his Saturday night business.

They waited. It seemed like a long time but probably was not.

"This one," Red whispered as another drunk stumbled near after leaving Tambor's. "Yeah. This guy is shit-faced. C'mon."

Red led the way, slipping out from behind the barrels a split second after their intended victim passed them. He stepped in behind the drunk and raised his homemade cosh — a leather pouch filled with lead birdshot; the three had spent several afternoons after school working on these projects — and rapped the drunk behind the left ear.

The man went down in the dirt face-first. For a moment Danny had the terrified thought that the man was dead.

The fellow grunted. And began to snore.

Red grinned. "See? Easy as that." He knelt and began pawing through their victim's pockets.

"What about . . . ?"

"Hush. We gotta move fast. Clean him out and skedaddle. Tomorrow he'll think he spent all his money or lost it, but we don't want anybody to see us here. Now, help me with this guy. Help me turn him so's I can get to his other pocket. He's lying on top o' the damn thing."

Red reached into that pocket too, then with a grin handed Henry a handful of coins. "Let's go. But don't be dropping none of those, you hear?"

The three jumped to their feet and scampered, running light and swift into the night.

Lordy, but this was exciting!

3

Eastern Kansas 1877

"Well, ain't you purty," Red teased in an exaggerated drawl.

"Don't start up now," Danny warned. "I may be fancy but I'm plenty mean."

Red laughed and pulled out a twist of molasses-soaked tobacco. He gnawed off a chunk and offered the soggy twist to Danny, who gave him a dirty look and went back to examining himself in the mirror.

Danny was as stiff in the heavy suit his mother had sewed for him as if the cloth were spun from strands of steel instead of wool. She had found a boiled shirt that was three sizes too large, and the mismatched bat-wing collar chafed his throat and kept him from lowering his chin. He doubted he would be able to see his feet if his shoes caught on fire.

"Can I ask you something, Red?"

"Sure. You can always ask. Might be I'll

answer." Red grinned. "Maybe even tell the truth if I do." The grin became wider. "Or not."

"What I was wondering . . . are you sorry you . . . you know."

"Quit school? Naw. That's all right for you fellas but I never much cared for it t' begin with."

"I sure wisht you was gonna be there to get your diploma along with Henry and me."

"That's fine of you, Danny, but I got no regrets. None at all."

"That's good. I'm glad."

"The reason I come by this morning is to ask you to come over to my place this evening. I'll be asking Henry too of course." Ever since Red's father died, almost a year before, the threesome had abandoned their hangout by the creek and got together in the shack Red had shared with his father. Red laughed. "If you *gentlemen* aren't too hoity-toity to be seen with the likes o' me, that is."

Danny pursed his lips and peered toward the ceiling for a moment. "I shall have to speak with my appointments secretary, but I don't know of any barrier to our attendance."

Red stood. "After commencement then.

Before the parties get started."

"What's up, fella?"

Red's smile was positively wicked. And smug at the same time. "You will see, my good man. You will see. Now, if you'll excuse me, I have to go find Henry."

Oh, the commencement was grand. One of the fire companies sent their band, complete with Mr. Clay Adams's oom-pah horn, to play the march onto the stage. Not that the procession was so very involved. There were just the three of them. Jessica Jones was the valedictorian. Henry was the salutatorian. And there was Danny. He supposed he was the student body.

Even so, the entire school and a good many townspeople, some of whom did not even have children, showed up for the ceremony. Jessica gave her speech. It was too long. Henry gave his. It was too short. And Danny squirmed in his seat. That damned collar was rubbing his throat raw. He figured he knew now what it felt like to be hanged.

They got through it though. Miss Addison handed out the sheepskins. Hands were shaken and congratulations offered. The obligatory jokes were cracked.

And they were officially adults. High

school graduates with the diploma to show for it. To show, that is, if one could pry the diploma away from Danny's mother. She swiftly appropriated his on their way out of the school building afterward. For safekeeping, she said. Danny figured she wanted to marvel at it as proof that she had done her motherly duty and gotten him somehow through the ordeal of growing up. Probably she was as surprised by this success as he was.

Danny and Henry followed Jessica outside into the bright glare of the afternoon sunshine, and Henry asked the dreaded question.

"So what are we gonna do now, Danny?"

School days were over and he had no answer to give Henry.

Danny was deeply touched. Red, who never picked up a piece of discarded clothing until toadstools were growing beneath it, had tidied his shack until Danny scarcely recognized it. There was even a blanket spread nice and smooth on top of the lumpy mattress, and there was a bottle of liquor and three mismatched glasses arrayed on the barrel head that served as a table.

A carefully lettered sign, painted in barn red, was propped on the rusty iron surface of the stove. It read: "Congraulation."

Spelling never had been Red's strong suit.

"A celebration," Red announced when both of his guests had taken their seats. "A celebration and a toast."

He uncorked the whiskey bottle and poured into all three glasses. "I know you're off the stuff," he said to Danny when he shoved the whiskey across the barrel to him, "so just take a sip for the toast."

Red served Henry and then himself. He raised his glass — it was real glass too and not a tin mug, although God knew where he found actual glassware — and said, "To the finest friends a fella ever had. Here's hoping the three of us stay like those Three Musketeers. Friends forever."

Red grinned. "Down the hatch, boys."

He very ceremoniously took a deep swallow of the whiskey and Henry did likewise. Danny tasted his. It was better than he remembered. He drank the remainder of his drink and was there when Red offered seconds.

"Daniel. Are you listening to me?"

"Yes, Ma. I'm listening." He wasn't. He had been up nearly the entire previous night, drinking with Red and Henry, and now he was hungover and peevish.

"I heard that Mr. Cooper needs a . . . needs someone to help him with deliveries."

"I already talked to him, Ma." That was the truth. He'd greeted Mr. Cooper good morning just the day before. Or the day before that. But he did talk to Mr. Cooper.

"What did he say, Daniel?"

"What?"

"Mr. Cooper. What did he say?"

"Oh. He'll, uh, he'll get back to me later."

"Well, while you're waiting to hear from him you should look with others too, you know. 'More irons in the fire' I believe is the expression the drovers used."

That piqued Danny's interest enough to make him actually sit upright and pay attention. "Tell me what they were like, Ma, those old-time cattle drovers."

"No! Absolutely not," his mother declared. "They were wild and wicked creatures, and the last thing in the world I would want would be for you to be like them."

"Do you think they'll ever come back here, Ma?"

"Of course not. We have laws now. They can go" — she waved her hand dismissively — "somewhere else. Not eastern Kansas. Never again."

"Yes'm." Danny stood, rubbing his eyes

and weaving just a mite unsteadily on his feet.

"Where are you going, Daniel?"

He shrugged. "Out."

"Be back by . . ." But he was already gone.

"Either of you guys want a trim?"

"Aw, c'mon, Henry. You already cut our hair so many times we look like sheep after they been sheared," Danny said.

"You think I'd let you near me with scissors again, son?" Red put in. "Not after what you done to me the last time."

"But I'm getting good at it. Really." He grinned. "Besides, you ought t' get to me while it's safe. Next week my pop is going to start teaching me how to give shaves."

"Jesus!" Danny said. "Preserve us from this idiot."

"C'mon, guys. I need to practice if I'm ever going to learn how to do this right."

"No chance, buddy. Danny, pour Henry another drink. Maybe that will shut him up."

"One for you," Danny said, tipping the whiskey bottle over Henry's tin cup. "And one for you. And finally . . . one more wee small one for me." He set the bottle down without bothering to cork it.

"Red, ol' boy, where're you getting all this crap?"

"What crap?"

Danny waved his hand. "This. You know. Liquor. Tobacco. Stuff. Where's it all come from? And don't tell me it comes from the store, smart-ass. I know you buy it, but where are you getting the money to treat us so good?"

"Are you sure you want t' know?"

"Yeah, buddy. I do."

"I steal."

"You aren't still rolling drunks are you?"

"Naw. That didn't pay much. By the time a guy gets passed-out drunk, he's already spent most of his money. Now I get them while they still got money in their overalls."

"You're the one the newspaper wrote about? The Payday Bandit?"

"That's me. I knock 'em in the head and lift their purses and nobody has any idea that it's me 'cause I don't flaunt my poke afterward." Red frowned. "Except since that damn story came out in the paper, all the stupid farm boys have got wise. They travel in twos and threes, most of them, even to go to the shitter." He laughed. "It's discouraging, I tell you."

"So what will you do now? Go back to rolling drunks?"

"Actually, I got an idea or two. But it'd take more than just me. I'd need help. Are you interested?"

"I might be." Danny scowled. "The only job I been able to find since we graduated school is shoveling shit at the livery, and that's only part-time. I could sure as hell use some real money."

"It would mean robbing. You should know that."

"But we wouldn't really hurt anybody, right?"

"Oh, hell no. Just take some money. An' from rich guys who can afford it. But we wouldn't hurt them."

"What about Henry?"

"I dunno. D'you think he'd rather stand around snipping scissors all day or go t' be a handsome, dashing bandito?"

"Dashing, anyway," Danny countered.

"Tell you what. We'll invite Henry t' join us. There's money enough for all if he wants to come in."

"Listen, if you guys are in, then so am I," Henry declared. "One for all and all for one, just like those musketeers. What do you have in mind?"

"Paley's Store. You heard of it?"

"I have," Henry said.

"Not me. What is it?"

"It's a store, dummy."

"Okay, it's a store. *Where* is it?"

"It's about ten miles east of here," Red said.

"More like twelve."

"Ten, twelve, who cares."

"And how are we supposed to go that far?" Danny asked.

Red grinned. "I got me a deal worked out with Jim Cooley, that's how."

"He's the old geezer that works at the livery, right?"

"Yeah. Danny's work buddy."

Danny scowled. Red said, "Anyhow, I got a deal worked with him. After Mr. Benton goes home at night, Cooley is in charge. I slip him a couple bucks every now an' then and he lets me take a horse and saddle for a little night ride."

"Do you think we could take three?"

"I'm sure of it if we pay him extra."

Danny nodded.

Red continued, "You know payday is the end of the month. All the farm boys come in an' pay off what they owe at the store, and from then until Paley drives into town to the bank he's got a whole shitpot full of money just setting there waiting for somebody to take it off him."

"First of the month, eh?"

"This month Sunday night the second. Everybody will've paid off their debts, but the bank won't be open for Paley to take the money in. Sunday night will be the best time to hit him."

"That sounds all right to me."

"Count me in too."

Red's grin grew wider than ever.

The only hard part was the ride out there, bouncing around on a clumsy farm horse that had a trot fit to break teeth. For a while Danny actually put the ends of his bandana in his mouth to keep his teeth from jamming together and chipping. He intended to remember that horse. And maybe shoot it. For sure he did not want to be stuck with that one again.

Once they reached Paley's, though, everything went just fine. It was late at night, and not another soul was around.

Red stepped down from his horse and nodded to Danny. In a loud whisper he said, "You hold the horses for us. Henry and me will go inside."

That was fine with Danny. He was feeling a little short of breath and fluttery in his gut. He nodded.

His eyes went wide when he saw Red pull

a revolver out of his britches.

"Where'd you get that? Man, you didn't say anything about shooting anybody."

"I'm not gonna shoot anyone. I got this off a drunk I rolled. I use it just to scare them."

"You've used a gun on people before?"

"Not *used,* dummy. Scared. There's a difference." Red grinned. "Don't fret y'self, Danny boy. Everything is gonna be all right. Your old pal Red is in charge, an' I know what I'm doing. Now, hold these horses. Henry and me will be back in five minutes."

Danny took the reins to all three animals. They left the cinches tight, as they would be needing to use those mounts in something of a hurry when the job was done.

Red and Henry went around the side of the building and out of Danny's sight. He knew what they would be doing there. There was a window. They intended to go in that way.

According to Red, the proprietor slept in the back. He was an old man, maybe in his fifties. Red said he was hard of hearing so they might be able to get in and out without ever waking him.

The horses fidgeted and stamped, picking up on Danny's nervousness.

He heard nothing from inside, but every

tiny night noise gave him a start. The others had been gone so long — or at least it felt like they were out of sight a long time — that he became convinced Red and Henry were discovered. Captured. Killed. Danny did not know whether he should take the horses and run or if he should try to go inside to see what was keeping them.

He almost wet himself when he heard the click of a latch and then a squeal from the hinges on the front door. It was only Henry who emerged, though, and Red a moment later. Red was carrying his pistol in hand. Henry had a small steel box tucked under his arm.

"Come on, boys, I think I heard Paley getting out o' bed. This would be a real good time to leave."

Danny stifled his questions. He distributed the reins, unsure of who was riding which animal but in a rush to get rid of them. He stepped into the saddle of his plow horse, a feeling of relief flowing through him and making him so weak in the knees that he had to try a second time to make it onto the saddle.

"Lordy, let's get outa here."

The ride back to Red's place was exhilarating. Danny's senses were heightened by the thrill of danger, of discovery. The night air was crisp. The stars and the moon were brighter and clearer than ever before. He could feel and rejoice in every ripple of motion in the horse beneath him. He would gladly have ridden like this forever.

They slowed to a walk well outside town and headed first to the livery, where they returned the horses.

"Psst," Danny hissed. "What about him?" He inclined his head toward Jim Cooley, who was in charge of the borrowed animals.

"Don't worry. I'll take care o' him later. Come along, you two. Let's us see what we got."

The three boys went through the alleys to reach Red's place, Red leading the way, Henry following close on Red's heels with Paley's cash box under his arm, and Danny bringing up the rear of their little late-night procession.

Once safely indoors, Red lighted a lamp and motioned for Henry to set the steel box onto the barrel-head table. "Let's see what we have here, boys. Give me a minute. I got a hammer around here someplace so's we can bust it open."

"Why don't we just open the latch?" Henry said.

"It ain't locked?"

"No."

"Then open it, quick."

Henry spilled a cascade of silver and copper coins — very little gold, though — onto the barrel head.

"Danny, you count for us."

"You want me to divide it up?" The jumble of heavy coins was just about the most money Danny had ever seen at one time. And it was theirs. So easy. It was theirs.

"Yeah, boy. Count it."

"You want me to divvy it up too?"

"Not yet. Just count it first. Then we'll take out some for Cooley." Red grinned. "*Then* we'll divvy it up."

"Jeez!" Danny was trembling with excitement when he began to count.

This robbery stuff . . . it was damn sure fun.

4

Eastern Kansas 1879

"I got me an idea," Red said, grinning.

Danny turned to Henry and poked him in the ribs. "Have you noticed? Whenever ol' Red gets that look on him, *we're* the ones who get in trouble."

"My pop hasn't forgiven me since the last time we were out, uh, playing."

"He doesn't know . . . ?"

"Oh, hell no. I wouldn't tell anybody about that."

"That's good. What were you saying, Red?"

"If you two idjits will pay attention for a minute, I was saying that I have an idea."

"For a job?"

"Yeah."

"Good, because it's been a couple months since the last money we collected and I'm near about broke."

"I can loan you some, Danny," Henry

said. "You know I don't spend much of what we take. I don't want my folks wondering where I've come up with money they can't account for."

"They aren't still giving you an allowance, are they? At your age?"

Henry did not answer. Which was in fact an answer.

"Are you boys gonna listen to what I have to say or ain't you?"

"I'm listening, Red."

"Me too. I'm all ears."

"You look like you're all ears, all right. Okay, now here's the deal. We'll do it this time before the first of the month. The twenty-ninth, I think. I'll kind of keep an eye on the bank to be sure, but I think the twenty-ninth. When he has cash on hand to pay his workers."

"A payroll? We're gonna take a whole payroll?"

"Just a small one." The grin returned. "Or maybe not so small."

"Won't it be guarded?"

"Not this payroll," Red said. "He goes to the bank just before the end of the month and draws out enough cash to pay his people."

"Who are we talking about here?"

"Mr. Lewis."

"Hey, we can't rob him. My mom works for him," Danny yelped.

"Shit, boy, I know that. We'll go in after your mom has gone home for the night."

"What about her pay? She can't afford to not get paid."

"Aw, he has plenty o' money. He'll just have t' go to the bank an' get more to replace what we take. Your mom won't be hurt none, and we ought t' take a shitpot o' money from Mr. Lewis."

"Man, I don't know."

"This ought to be the easiest job yet. No guards. No safe or anything like that. Just his little black satchel that he carries his payroll in every month. You've seen it, Danny. Seen it a hundred times. All we have to do is wait until your mom is gone and the house is quiet. Then we'll slip in the back door and ask Mr. Lewis nice an' polite to give us that satchel. Why, this time we won't even need to borrow any horses to get away. The deal is perfect. Trust me."

Over time — five robberies since Paley's store, including a second hit on Paley — the boys had perfected their disguises. Each of them had a flour sack that he tied over his head. The sacks had eye holes cut out of them and wild, garish faces painted on them. Each boy had decorated his own on a laughing, whiskey-soaked Saturday afternoon.

In addition to the masks, they wore long dusters that hid their clothing so they could not be identified by what they wore.

To ensure against accidental discovery by Danny's mother or one of Henry's parents, the disguises were all stored at Red's shack between thefts.

The evening of the twenty-ninth they rolled their disguises together into a bundle and carried them into a thicket of chokecherry behind Lewis's big house. They hid there and watched while first the cook, Mrs. Ramirez, left by way of the back door and then, it seemed a long time later, Danny's mother.

It gave Danny an odd feeling to see his mother like that, head down and humble, subservient to Lewis, whereas at home she was the unquestioned boss. Seeing her there gave him a pang of . . . he did not quite know what the feeling was . . . a tightening in his throat. Whatever that meant.

He shook off the discomfort and grimaced.

Red motioned for the others to lean closer to him and whispered, "All right. We'll wait another fifteen or twenty minutes, then go in. Here. Let's put our stuff on now."

Red parceled out the dusters and the flour sacks. Danny's sack had cat's whiskers drawn on it, Henry's large eyes and lips. Red's was decorated with fangs and thick eyebrows.

"Remember," Red said. "No talking in there. Not a word. It could be he'd recognize your voices. Whatever has t' be said, I'll say. I'll change my voice some. Not that he knows me anyhow, but better safe than sorry. Now sit tight until I signal. And remember. No talking. Not a word."

For some reason, perhaps because this house was where his mother worked, Danny was not feeling the thrill of excitement while they waited to go in. If anything, what he felt was a faint sense of dread. He leaned closer to Red and hissed to get Red's attention.

"Listen, are you sure . . ."

"Shh. No more talking. We'll go in now."

As always it was Red who led the way out of the thicket and silently onto the back porch. He tried the door — it was unlocked — and led the way inside.

They tiptoed from the clean and tidy kitchen, the cavernous room smelling of naphtha soap and hot water, into the hallway leading to the front of the house. Danny's heart leaped into his throat when a floorboard creaked underfoot, and Red laid a cautionary finger over the place where his mouth would be under the mask.

Red seemed to be heading for the parlor at the very front of the house. A glow of lamplight spilled out of that room into the entry hall.

They were nearly there when immediately beside them another door opened. Danny had thought the door was a closet. Apparently it was a water closet, an indoor facility so the rich would not have to go outdoors in bad weather to shit.

Danny thought his heart would jump completely out of his mouth to be confronted without warning like that.

Then he noticed that Mr. Lewis was bringing something out of his pocket. Something bright and shiny. A pistol. Oh, God!

"Hold it right there, you. All of you. I will shoot if I have to. I mean it."

Danny froze. So did Henry behind him.

Not Red.

Red, in the lead, had already gone past the door where Mr. Lewis had popped out and surprised them. Red whirled. He clamped a hand on Lewis's wrist and bore down.

Grunting with effort and straining, Red punched Lewis in the neck and shoved him back inside the tiny water closet.

Danny stood, transfixed, for the first time in one of their exploits truly frightened.

Red and Lewis disappeared into the water closet. All Danny could see of them was the back of Red's pale duster and the back of his head.

He could hear them though. Thumping and banging. Lewis shouting. Red snarling for him to shut up. Grunts of effort and groans of pain. And then, then a sharp bang.

The loud, abrupt bang of the pistol discharging, and Red said, "Oh, shit, boys. Oh, dammit to hell."

There was one more final thump as Avery Lewis fell onto the polished oak seat of his shitter.

"Oh, just dammit t' hell, boys."

Red was holding Lewis's pistol in his hand when he emerged from the water closet.

"I swear to God I didn't mean to do it," Red moaned for probably the tenth time.

They were back at Red's shack. They'd run straight there from the Lewis mansion, bolting out the back way and fleeing as if for their lives. They had not taken time to look for Mr. Lewis's payroll satchel. Just

67

turned and ran.

Danny was still trembling. Red seemed calm to all outward appearance, but over the years Danny had learned that he could not always read his friend's emotions.

He had no such difficulty with Henry. No sooner had they arrived in the safety of Red's cabin, Henry bolted back outside and puked in the scrub that was growing unchecked beside the porch. Danny felt a little like throwing up himself.

Mr. Lewis was *dead*.

They hadn't wanted that. Had not intended it.

Somehow — for some reason — Red had shot him. And it had not been an accident. That was plain enough to see. The bullet that killed him entered his face just below his right eye. That must have been deliberate.

Danny wanted to ask Red about that. He was afraid to. He did not really want to know the answer to that question. Not now. Not ever.

"Ever" was a very long time, but one thing Danny was sure of. He would "ever" have the image of Mr. Lewis's dead body in his mind. He had glanced in only for a moment and recoiled in horror. The old man lay crumpled atop his oak commode, his trou-

sers stained dark where he'd pissed himself
as he died, his face misshapen by the bullet
that shattered it. And blood. Blood running
in bright rivulets down the side of the
polished wood.

No, that was a sight he expected never to
forget.

"Boys, we're in for it now," Red said
darkly. "We're murderers an' robbers an'
we are in for it now."

Danny shuddered. Life, he was sure,
would never be simple again.

"Skedaddle, that's what we've got t' do.
We're gonna be suspected. You know we are.
Something as bad as this happens, folks are
gonna wonder about the three of us, helling
around like we do. An' this time it's no
penny-ante bullshit. This time it's murder,
boys. They hang people for murder."

"Oh, God."

"Call out to God if you like. But if you
got any sense, you'll be doing it from the
back of a fast horse."

"What about kit? Where will we go? How
are we supposed to get horses?"

"We'll steal the horses. Them we can take
from the livery stable. We'll take them the
same as usual. It's just that we won't be
bringing them back this time. An' we'll take

whatever money we've got stuffed away someplace. Henry, you said you still have a lot o' your share put by. Well, now's the time to bring it out. It's share an' share alike, boys. Now, what all are we gonna need to live on the run?"

"The horses and saddles, of course."

"We as good as got those."

"Guns. If we're gonna be on the run, we got to be able to defend ourselves. We need guns."

"We'd best buy those. Can't count on being able to steal guns. After all, the guy who has them to rob off him just might wanta shoot instead of giving them up, and all we got to face anybody with is that little lady gun thing Mr. Lewis had. I say we use some of whatever money we got to buy guns."

"This pissy little thing was good enough to kill Lewis though, wasn't it?" Red said, pulling the nickel-plated revolver from his pocket and looking it over. He broke open the action, removed the empty cartridge cases and tossed them aside. With a shrug and a grin he said, "No point in being tidy, I reckon. We're gonna light outa here and never come back anyhow."

"I don't like this," Henry said.

"Nobody likes it, Henry, but Red is right. Soon as that old man's body is discovered, somebody is sure to think it was us. We got to get away from here lest we hang." Danny could feel a tightening in his throat at the mere thought of being hanged.

"What are you gonna tell your mom, Danny?"

"Nothing. I'm not gonna tell her nothing. Just take up my blankets like I was gonna lay out in the woods with you guys and walk out the door. If I'm lucky, she'll be over at the neighbor's gossiping and I won't have to tell her a damn thing."

"What about you, Henry? Are you all right with this?"

"All right with it? Hell no, I'm not all right with it. But it's what we got to do if we don't want to hang."

"Don't tip it off by telling your folks good-bye or anything stupid like that, Henry. Just slip your money in your pocket and take up your blankets like Danny said, just like we was going off down the creek fishing or something. Go on now, the both of you. We'll meet at the livery in fifteen minutes."

"Lordy, I hope we're doing the right thing."

"Hell, boy, it's already way too late t' do the right thing. Now we got t' do the best we can. There ain't nothing else left to us. It's down to either run or hang, an' me, I choose t' run."

"Then let's have us some fun until they take us down, dammit."

"One for all . . ."

". . . and all for one."

They managed a laugh as Danny and Henry were on their way out. But the truth was, Danny's insides felt like they had gone sour and curdled, and he did not much feel like laughing.

5

Western Kansas 1879

The three drew rein in front of a saloon in a town that was all mud and raw lumber. There was not a structure in the place that looked like it was more than five months old. That would have been about the start of the cattle droving season.

Red dismounted and looked warily around. "Loosen your cinches, boys. We ain't gonna do anything here but eat an' drink an' have us a real good time."

Whenever a robbery was planned — and in the past few weeks they had pulled off three fairly good hauls without having to fire a shot — they were careful to keep their cinches tight, ready for a fast ride away from pursuit.

They had also swapped horses several times during those weeks and now had three that they liked. Danny was riding a soft-mouthed, easygoing sorrel. Red had a tough, leggy black and Henry a short-coupled seal brown.

They were outfitted with revolvers, every one of them firing cartridges rather than cap and ball, and Spencer carbines. Winchesters would have been preferable, but army surplus Spencers were cheap and plentiful, while the Winchesters were harder to come by. Their Colts had army markings on them too and likely had been sold by deserters who took the guns with them when they ran away.

"Do you want should we bring our carbines inside?" Henry asked as they tied their mounts to the hitch rail and loosened the latigos.

"Hell, no. Nobody'd steal them," Red snapped. He was already in a cranky mood, had been all day long, and he seemed to resent the fact that they were carrying cheap guns.

"You don't think there would be a posse or something chasing us, do you?" Henry asked, looking back the way they had just come.

"From that shitty little place? Not damn likely." Their last robbery had been two days and fifty miles ago, and there probably had not been any sort of lawman within another fifty miles beyond that. "Come on, boys.

It's time we set down and have some fun."
Red's grin flashed, the first they had seen of
that all day long.

Red led the way into the cool shadows of
the saloon. The place smelled of spilled beer
and chalk dust. There were no permanent
games in play, no roulette or anything
requiring special equipment, but there were
three tables where a man could play cards if
he liked, and there was a billiards table and
rack of cues.

The bar was made of rough planks laid
over barrel heads. A beer barrel was propped
rather precariously atop a scaffolding of raw
wood, and there were smaller kegs for hard
spirits. Mugs were made of pewter or perhaps tin. There was nothing visible in the
place that would be easily breakable.

Red stopped, inhaled deeply and smiled.
"Mother, I'm home," he called out.

The bartender smiled too. But then he
likely knew a good customer when he saw
one.

"Will you two for Chris'sakes pick your eyes
back up off the floor an' stuff them back in
your heads where they belong?" Red complained. "Haven't you ever seen a whore
before?"

"Uh . . . no. I haven't," Danny admitted.

"Me neither," Henry said.

"Of course you have. Miz Thompson back home."

"The widow, lives over by George Leamon?"

"That's the one. She'll haul a man's ashes for fifty cents. Makes out pretty good on Saturday nights. And that skinny black girl that lives off the alley behind Pullman's store, she'll do it for a quarter."

"Are you sure about this?"

"Damn right, I am. I know. I been with them both."

"You never told us that."

"I don't tell you everything, Danny-boy," Red said, laughing. "Come on. We got money. Let's see if they want some of it."

"Are you talking about our money," Henry asked, "or, um . . . ?"

Danny laughed. But he surely was nervous all of a sudden.

"Everybody calls me Ruby, so if you ask for me sometime you should ask for Ruby. But my real name is Jenny." She had big, trusting eyes and bad teeth, and she was so pretty that Danny was about to damn burst.

His breath came short and he could feel his heart racing. He was a little bit light-headed and woozy.

"What's your name, honey?"

He told her, although he stumbled over the sounds getting them out of his mouth.

"Would you like to go with me, honey?"

Danny nodded.

"It will be a dollar."

"I thought it was only fifty cents."

"Oh, honey, you aren't going to haggle, are you?" Her smile became even wider, although he would not have thought that possible. "Do you have a dollar, honey?"

"I got a dollar. Sure I do."

"Well?"

"I, uh, do I pay you now or in the room?"

"Now would be good, honey."

He handed her the money and floated slightly off the floor when he followed Jenny through a curtain to a dark, tiny room in the back of the saloon.

Once there, he was hoping she would get naked. Like Sallie Benson used to do. Now Sallie was married and gone off somewhere. Now Danny was with a girl named Jenny. He hoped he did not unload in his trousers. That would be awful. He was . . . maybe he was just the least little bit nervous.

"Come on, honey. What did you say your name was again?" Jenny hiked her skirts up around her waist and lay on the narrow cot in the room. She parted her legs but it was too dim in there for Danny to get a really good look at what girls are like down there.

Oh, but . . . Lordy . . . he could certainly *feel* what it was like.

It was the warmest, nicest, most wonderful thing he had ever felt. Better than he had imagined.

Lordy!

"Don't you two look like the cats that ate the canary," Red snorted when Henry and Danny both emerged from the back rooms where Danny had been with Jenny and Henry with a fat blond girl. There were only the two girls working, so Red had remained at the bar while the others got their first taste of what it was all about.

"Have a good time, did you?"

"Let me tell you, I did," Henry crowed. "Oh, she'll remember me, she will." Henry proceeded to describe in some detail exactly what he had done and how he had done it. According to him he was quite the bull.

"What about you, Daniel?" Red asked when Henry finally wound down.

Danny only smiled and took a sip of beer.

"Texas," Danny said. "All my life I've heard about Texas. I want to see it before I die, and we got no better of a idea than that. I say we head south from here."

"What about you, Henry? You got a better idea than Danny's?"

"Hell, Texas is fine with me." Henry wiped his mouth and grinned. "But I wanta tear me off another piece o' ass first."

"You're ready for seconds this soon?"

"Damn right I am."

"Well, I haven't had firsts yet," Red said. "You in a hurry t' go again, Danny?"

He stretched his legs out and crossed them at the ankles. "You fellas go ahead. I'll have me another beer. If you aren't done by the time I finish it, I'll go on down the street and do some shopping. I seen a sign for a shoemaker, and I think it's time I buy a proper pair of boots. We ain't in such a hurry that I can't get me some boots made up, are we? It shouldn't take but a couple days."

Henry leaned close and whispered, "What about a posse?"

"Jesus, Henry, there's no damn posse after us, so don't get yourself all lathered up over nothing. Now tell me. D'you want the fat girl again or d'you wanna try the one Danny was with? What'd you say her name is, Danny?"

"Je—" He remembered at the last moment that she was not supposed to be called that here, that she had told him her real name. That made him feel mighty good. "Ruby," he said. "Her name is Ruby."

"She any good? Never mind I asked that. The way you're acting, she must be. Well, Henry? Which one d'you want?"

"I'll stick with Kate if you don't mind."

"It's all the same t' me," Red said, shoving back from the table and heading for the bar, where the two whores were talking with the barman.

6

Cherokee Nation, Indian Territory 1883
Danny sat up, stretching and yawning and rubbing the sleep out of his eyes. The other boys were still sleeping, Red curled into a tight ball atop his bunk and Henry snoring fit to rattle the rafters. He slid his feet into his boots and stood. He shook his head and rubbed his eyes again, then walked softly to the door of the dugout, hoping not to wake either of the others.

Morning was the best time of day. Clean. Clear. Full of promise. Danny eased the door shut behind him and shivered a little in the predawn chill.

He walked the few paces to the corral and checked the horses. A dark head lifted, ears pricked, and whickered softly. "It's all right, boy. Go back t' your hay."

Danny picked up the pail of water that always sat at the base of the pump. He poured half of it down the spout to prime the pump, then began rhythmically pulling the sweet, cold water from the ground. He refilled the pail first and returned it to its place, then the trough for the animals, and finally plunged his own head and shoulders under the flow.

"Jesus! That's cold," he muttered aloud. But it felt good nonetheless.

He smoothed his hair back with both hands and shivered some more.

Overhead the sky was dark, but off to the east there were hints of purple to suggest that dawn would not be long in coming. The day promised to be a fine one.

Danny stopped to gather an armload of split wood off the pile, then went back inside to light the stove and put a pot of coffee on. It was his turn today to cook.

"I'm getting tired of laying around like this," Red complained.

Danny knew what would come next.

"Besides, we're running low on money," Red said, grinning. "It's time we go get us some more."

"Where to this time?" Henry asked.

The old dugout they rented from an elderly Osage man was just about perfectly situated. In the various Indian territories there was virtually no law for white men to worry about, and from the Cherokee Nation they could easily ride east into Arkansas, angle northeast to Missouri or travel north to Kansas.

And over the years they had learned. The large and dangerous gangs robbed banks and railroad cars, collected large hauls . . . and had grimly determined posses chasing them.

Danny and his friends had no headlines or notoriety the way the more famous gangs did, and their proceeds were more likely to be counted in the hundreds of dollars rather than thousands.

They made a living by robbing isolated country stores or waylaying the occasional traveler. Rent collection agents making their rounds at the end of the month were an especially easy target and a surprisingly lucrative one.

The money came easy and went out just as quickly, but the whiskey and the women were a joy.

And no one lives forever.

"I know where I want to go," Danny said.

"Where's that?"

"Home."

"Did I hear that right?"

"You did. Look, Red, I know you don't have any people still living there, but Henry and me do. On our way north we could swing over and see our folks. Just for a visit. See how they're getting along."

"We're wanted there," Red protested.

"Maybe. Hell, we don't know that. Could be nobody blamed us for that shooting. Nobody saw us. Anyway, it's been four years. They will've forgot all about us by now. An' I know I'd like to see my ma. Henry?"

Henry nodded. "I'd like to stop in and see my folks. Just to, you know, let them know we're all right."

"Come on, Red. You can stay with me and my mother if that's what is worrying you."

"The hell with that. I won't have any trouble finding some little pump-ass whore to keep company with while you children are getting your faces scrubbed an' your asses paddled. Listen, if you want to chuck this whole thing an' go back to your mamas, you just say the word." Red looked peeved.

"That isn't what I'm saying. Henry neither. We just want to, well, to see how our people are. Tell them we're all right. They're probably worrying, you know. We could stop in just for a little while. A day maybe. It would ease their minds."

"You don't want t' break up the gang?"

Danny grinned. He pointed to the hovel

where they had been living and said, "And give up all this splendor?"

"Just for one day?" Red asked.

"I'd sure like that," Henry said.

Red was silent for a few moments. Then he nodded. "All right. We'll swing by home. Then back east. Hit a couple places on the way. Maybe ride over into Missouri an' hit some more. When we have enough money in our pokes to make it worthwhile, we'll come back here again."

Danny felt oddly excited by the prospect of seeing his mother again. He wondered how she was getting by. If he had some money he could spare, he would leave some with her. That was it. He would leave some money for her.

He felt good once he had decided that.

The ride home took four days. They could have made it in three, but on their way out to a job they never pushed the horses hard. They knew they might need the animals' speed and endurance for a swift getaway afterward. As it was, it was evening and getting dark before they reached the town.

Little seemed to have changed. There were a few more houses and an expanded wagon yard behind the livery, but other than that the town seemed very much the same as when they left.

By unspoken consent they avoided riding past the house where Avery Lewis had lived. Danny wondered though. Who lived there now? Did his mother still work there? And the biggest question of all: Had anyone made the connection between Mr. Lewis's murder and their disappearance? Perhaps now they would get the answer to that. He just hoped it was not something they learned the hard way.

Red drew rein in the once familiar territory behind the livery and said, "We'll split up here. Henry, you go on and see your folks. Danny and me will ride around and come in behind his place. We'll meet up again tomorrow morning."

"No!" Danny said sharply.

"What d'ya mean 'no'?"

"Just what I said, dammit. No, we're not gonna meet up at dawn tomorrow and ride away again that quick. That isn't time enough to visit." Danny looked to Henry for support and got an affirming nod of agreement. Henry usually sided with Red whenever he and Danny disagreed, but not this time. Henry wanted time to visit with his family too.

"When then?"

"Day after tomorrow. Dawn, just like you

said, but the day after tomorrow."

Red grinned. "You're the one said dawn. Me, I just said we'd meet in the morning. Hell, if I find some little whore that can bounce her butt nice an' fast, I might not be wanting t' crawl out of the sack at dawn. Might want to stay long enough to get me another piece before I'm ready to ride off with you boys."

"Morning the day after tomorrow then. Just *past* dawn. Does that suit everybody?" Danny asked.

"It sure as hell suits me."

"All right, Henry, we'll see you then. Danny, let's go. I haven't had a drink all day and I'm getting thirsty."

They stopped outside the fence that ran behind Danny's mother's property. "Okay, Red. Where you gonna be flopping? I got t' know so I know where to come grab you and drag your scrawny ass out."

"I'll take a room over the saloon. You know."

Each started off in his own direction, but Red stopped and turned back. "We been gone a long time, Danny. Give your ma a little time to adjust t' having you back. Y'know?"

"Sure. Thanks, Red."

Red went sauntering off through the alley, whistling and carrying his Winchester repeater jauntily over one shoulder.

Danny stopped outside the gate leading into the tiny yard where his mother used to do her washing. He stood there for long moments, heart pounding and breath coming short. Funny. He was not this nervous when he was the inside man on a stickup.

Finally gathering his nerve, he tugged the gate open. It swung wide with no protest of squealing hinges the way it always used to. Someone had been greasing the metal. Danny stepped into the yard.

He was nearly bowled over by a small boy who ran full tilt into him.

"Hey!"

The kid did fall down. Immediately he scrambled to his feet and scampered onto the porch shouting something in a language Danny did not understand.

A doe-eyed girl of eight or so peeped out of the back door. That door too opened silently, without squealing. The child looked, then popped back inside the protection of the house.

Moments later Danny's mother came out, surrounded by three children — the boy, the girl and another girl — who clung to her skirts. Danny's mother wore a nearly new housedress and a clean, white apron. She had aged more than Danny would have believed had he not seen it for himself.

The thing that most surprised him was that there was no flush of welcome on her lined old face.

The first words out of her mouth were "I got nothing for you, Daniel. Nothing."

Danny poured a shot into his beer and stirred the resulting mixture with his finger. Abruptly he tossed the drink back, then called for another.

"Hey, slow down, kid." Red leaned close, worry furrowing his brow. "You're gonna be all right, but slow down or you're gonna have a humdinger of a hangover tomorrow."

"Who gives a shit," Danny grumbled.

"So what's the deal with your mom, anyhow?"

"Oh, she's just fine. Plenty fine. She's taken up with some foreign son of a bitch. Basque, whatever that is." Danny scowled at his friend. "You got any idea what one of them is?"

"Never heard of 'em," Red said.

"She isn't married to this funny-talking prick, mind. She's just taken to living with him an' his kids. Says she knows I been in trouble an' there's no place for me there now."

"Sure, well, don't you worry about it. We got our own place, right? Right, Danny?" Red took him by the shoulder and lightly shook him. "We got our own thing going, buddy. Here. Have you another beer an' shooter, eh."

Danny reached for the fresh beer and shot.

7

Eastern Colorado 1884

The three sprawled in sun-dappled comfort beside a dry streambed, shaded by a stand of young cottonwoods. Red had half of a black cheroot dangling from his lips. Henry was smoking his pipe. Their horses were sleek and well rested, browsing now along a picket rope that was strung between two of the more sturdy trees.

Danny stood, looked toward the west, and shook his head. He sat back down. "Nothing."

"They'll be along. Count on it."

From their half-hidden vantage point they had an unobstructed view for miles east or west and almost as far north or south. The land here was nearly flat, sere and brown, covered with the short grasses and button cactus of the southern plains.

The rumor Red had picked up from one of his women was that the bank in Pueblo would be sending a shipment of cash to a bank in Grand Prairie, Kansas. It was considerate of the bank to bring the money to them. This time they would not have to bestir themselves to go after it.

"Anybody hungry?" Red asked. "We might be in too much of a hurry to stop an' cook later on."

"We're in too much of a hurry to cook right now," Henry said, shading his eyes and peering off to the west. "I think I see them coming."

All three stood and watched for a moment. There was definitely a vehicle of some sort headed their way. A few minutes later they could make it out as a light coach, a mud wagon.

"That should be it," Red said.

As one they turned and picked up their blankets and saddles, quietly settling those onto their horses and pulling their cinches tight.

There was no hurry. The coach would not reach them for another fifteen or twenty minutes. But they wanted to be ready.

The three drifted into position with the comfort of long practice, easing out from the shelter of the cottonwoods as the wagon came near. Their flour-sack clown masks were over their heads and their dusters buttoned to their throats. The horses were all plain, without markings or noticeable brands. Danny and Henry carried short-barreled shotguns held across their saddle bows. They could hit quickly and just as quickly dash away.

Danny and Red separated, flanking the roadway and allowing the wagon to come to them. Henry rode around behind the wagon.

"You know what this is, boys," Red called out to the two men who were riding atop the mud wagon. "Stand and deliver and no one gets hurt."

The driver was an older man. He looked peeved but not especially upset. The fellow beside him with the Winchester by his knees had a twitch in one eye and was nervously licking his lips beneath a straggly mustache.

"You boys hit me oncet before," the driver said. "Can't say as I appreciate you doin' me a second time."

"Sorry, neighbor, I don't remember you," Red said.

Danny did, but he never spoke aloud during their robberies. Neither did Henry. Red did all the talking for the group. But then Red was good at disguising his voice so that even his mother would not have recognized it.

"You know what we want. Toss it down," Red ordered.

"It's inside. You'll have t' fetch it yourselves."

Red motioned to Danny, then pointed toward the mud wagon. Danny nodded.

He nudged his horse close to the side of the wagon and leaned down to swing the door open, then stepped from saddle to wagon and swung inside.

A steel lockbox was bolted to the floor of the wagon.

Bolted!

Danny stuck his head out the door to motion Red toward him.

He felt the rig lurch as one of the horses bolted.

Danny felt himself falling. Too fast and unexpectedly for him to do anything about it.

He lost his balance and toppled out of the coach.

He heard more than felt the dull impact when he hit the ground.

Very dimly he heard shouting and gunfire.

He felt the blow and heard a low crunch as the back wheel of the wagon rolled over his chest.

More shouts. More shots.

He felt dizzy and his vision became blurred and tinged with red.

Danny heard Red and Henry and the old driver cursing and then more gunfire.

A darkness enveloped him and carried him gently away.

His mouth tasted of puke and bile, and his head felt like it was full of cotton wool. Fire engulfed his chest and his ears were ringing.

"Danny! Dammit, Danny."

The voice came from very far away.

Gradually he became a little more aware of his surroundings. He was lying facedown in the dirt, and he could smell sun-heated dust and sharp, acid vomit.

"You with us, buddy? Are you still with us?"

"Don't die, Danny." That voice was Henry. The first must have been Red. It seemed odd that he could have forgotten. And he hadn't. Exactly. He was just a little confused, that was all.

He opened his eyes. It was not an improvement.

Red's and Henry's boots were close to his shoulders. They seemed to be hunkering next to him.

95

"He's coming around, Red."

"I can see that. Danny! Wake up, Danny."

One of them touched his shoulder and lightly shook him, trying to waken him. The resulting feeling was like having swords shoved into his chest and twisted. He screamed.

"Jesus, Danny. Don't do that."

"You gonna puke again, Danny?"

He became aware that he no longer wore the flour-sack clown mask that he had used for years. It lay in the dirt beside him. Obviously Red or Henry had used it to try to clean his face after he threw up all over himself. He stank. And hurt. Oh, Lordy, how he hurt.

"Danny, you gotta get up. You got to ride. We gotta get away from here."

"We shot that messenger, Danny. God help us, we did," Henry wailed.

For their entire career as robbers the three had tried to avoid actually shooting anyone. Ever since they killed Avery Lewis. They had fired their revolvers to frighten, not to kill, and they waved their shotguns around but never fired those. And now . . . this.

"What else could we do, Danny? The sonuvabitch was trying to shoot you. So we shot him. Then the team jumped and . . . you know."

Danny nodded. He felt like puking again. He did gag a little, but nothing more came up. Probably there was nothing more in him *to* come up.

"You're busted up bad, Danny, but we got to get you on your horse. There'll be a posse along after us quick as the wagon driver gets anyplace to raise one. We got to skedaddle, Danny."

"We're gonna try an' get you on your horse, Danny."

They tried. Red and Henry picked Danny up at the shoulders and tried to lift him.

He screamed. The pain was unbearable. It felt like his insides were being torn apart, like some ugly monster was devouring him alive.

Red and Henry dropped him back onto the road.

"Danny, we got to . . . we got to . . ."

He felt himself being lifted again. His feet this time. And dragged. They dragged him across the dry, brittle grass and button cactus and into the shade of the cottonwoods where they had hidden waiting for the express wagon to come to them.

His friends dragged him to what shelter there was. They laid him out on the leaf-littered ground beside the old streambed, and they made him as comfortable as they could. He was far from being comfortable, but he understood.

"We got t' go, Danny. I'd stay here if I thought it'd do the least lick o' good, but you're dyin', Danny, and that posse is gonna be coming. We got t' go, buddy."

"Is there anything . . . Do you want your pistol so's you can shoot yourself when the pain gets too bad, Danny?"

"No . . . thanks . . . boys." A whisper was the best he could manage, and at that he thought the effort would tear his broken body in two.

"Look . . . Danny . . . if you don't mind, we'll go ahead an' take your horse. He's a good one, and we might need a spare if the chase runs long. You know how it is."

Danny managed a nod. It hurt, but he managed it.

"Yeah, well . . . all right then."

"We'll, uh, we'll see you, buddy."

Danny heard the shuffle of their boots as they walked away. The creak of leather and jangle of bit chains when they mounted. Finally the sound of the horses starting off at a walk and quickly lifting to a lope.

After that he heard nothing but the rustle of leaves overhead and felt nothing but the kiss of the breeze.

8

Eastern Colorado 1884

A wave of cold fear approaching panic washed through him from the nape of his neck down his spine. Something, some wild creature, was approaching.

He could hear the feet scuffling in the leaf litter. Then he could hear the animal's breathing.

Danny felt the light brush of hot breath on his ear.

And then a cold, wet nose against his cheek. What the . . . ?

The dog barked and went dashing away.

Danny's relief was so great he almost wet himself.

The dog barked. Ran back. Barked some more.

Danny could hear the approach of voices. Human voices.

His fear returned.

The posse. They were coming.

It was not bad enough that he would be fated to lie there and die a lonely death. Now it seemed he would be hanged instead. Jesus!

When they lifted him, he thought he would die. The pain shocked and terrified him. He had not known it was possible to hurt so very much. Or for it to continue for so very long.

He tried to wrench himself away from their grasp. That only made the pain worse.

He tried begging. They ignored him.

They . . . a man and two husky women wearing babushkas . . . picked him up by the arms and legs and carried him out of the woods to a handcart piled high with canvas-covered bales.

Working together, they muscled him atop the bales and tied him in place there. Then the two women picked up the cart tongue and began to pull.

The cart had no springs. Every bump jolted him. Every tiny obstruction in the road sent pain shooting into Danny's body.

He cried. He begged them to put him down and allow him to die. The man, the women and the dog ignored him. But then none of them seemed to speak English.

Eventually Danny passed out again.

■ ■ ■ ■

Danny recognized the stagecoach relay station. He had stopped there several times in the past, he and the others, stopping to eat and to pick up hints that might lead to their next robberies. Likely the mud wagon they'd tried to rob had been there early this morning.

The women dragged the cart up to the front of the low-roofed, sod-walled station and set the tongue down surprisingly gently. He hadn't thought they cared or even noticed that he was being jostled until his insides felt like they were being torn apart.

Once the bouncing stopped, the relief was so great he could have passed out from sheer pleasure.

Another relief was not so welcome. Lying out in the open for hours, crushed and possibly dying, then being pounded by that accursed cart while tied in place, he was no longer able to hold his water. A warm flood filled his britches and brought a flush of shame to his face. If the women and their male companion noticed they did not let on. The women stood stoically beside the cart while the man went inside.

A moment later the station keeper came

out. Danny searched his memory for the man's name. Kenneth something. He did not believe he'd ever heard the rest of it.

"I remember you. Dan Southern, isn't it? What'd you do, come off your horse? Get busted up some? Cat got your tongue?"

"H'lo, Kenneth." It came out as a whisper. That was the best he could do.

"What we're gonna do, boy, is lift you down off there and carry you inside. You ready?"

"No." But they ignored him.

All four, the two heavyset women, the nearly mute man and Kenneth, untied him and brought him down off the bales. Carefully, gently, they took him inside and laid him on the long communal dining table.

"Rest there, Dan. I'll be right back."

Danny's rescuers left before he had a chance to thank them. Not that he was entirely sure there was anything to thank them for. They may well have saved him from the wolves and the coyotes only to give him over to a hangman.

When Kenneth came back, his young wife was with him.

Kenneth was a lean man in his thirties. His wife — Danny thought her name was Anne — was barely out of her teens. They had an infant, but Danny did not know if the little one was a boy or a girl. He did know that Kenneth had lost his first wife and little boy to the cholera a few years earlier. He'd never met them, but he had heard about them.

"We're gonna bandage you up, Dan."

"I ain't bleeding, Kenneth."

"No, but your ribs are busted all to hell an' gone . . . excuse the language, dear . . . so you got to be taped up. Real tight. So tight it'll be hard for you to breathe. But it's got to be done lest things get to shifting around in there and cause you some serious hurt. Now, hold on to my hands. I'm gonna pull you up so you're sitting on the edge of the table."

The thing Danny was most conscious of was the wet and now miserably cold feel of his urine-soaked pants. The feel and the idea of what the dark stain must look like to Kenneth's missus.

That embarrassment was almost welcome as a distraction from the sharp spears of agony that shot through him when Kenneth pulled him upright with Anne pushing from behind.

Danny gritted his teeth to keep from crying out at the pain, but he could not help but groan aloud, and bright, salty tears rolled down his cheeks from the hurting.

They managed to get him into a sitting position, though, and Anne very carefully peeled Danny's shirt off.

"You're near about purple, you're so bruised," Kenneth observed.

"You ought t' try it from this side o' my skin," Danny whispered.

"Hold still now. This is going to hurt pretty bad."

Before Anne finished the first wrap with her heavy linen bandage, Danny's head went light and fuzzy and the pain diminished.

After a bit he felt nothing at all.

". . . and that's what happened," Danny lied.

He and Kenneth were seated in rocking chairs on the porch attached to the front of the relay station. Anne and the baby — after three days Danny still was not sure if the little critter was boy or girl — were inside preparing food for them and for however many folks might, or might not, show up when the next stage came through.

"Damned shame," Kenneth commiserated. "I'm just surprised your horse hasn't turned up anyplace."

Danny worked up a scowl. "Horse thief, d'you think?"

"Not likely," Kenneth said. "More prob'ly

whoever found him thought he was strayed and took him in. He'll show up. I'm sure of it."

Not if my luck holds, Danny silently thought. "I hope so because I'm afoot as it is."

"Dan, it's gonna be a spell before you're up to riding again anyway. Let those ribs heal. They haven't hardly started yet."

He managed a grin. "I think I knew that a'ready. They tell me so every time I try an' move."

"You want another teaspoon of laudanum?"

"Hell, Kenneth, I want another pint of the stuff. But, yeah, another spoonful would be awful nice. It takes the edge off the hurting. You know?"

"Aye, I do. Last time I got busted up, that was the only thing kept me from blowing my brains out." The man grinned. "Such as they are. Stay here. I'll go tell Anne to bring you the little brown bottle and a spoon." Kenneth stood and lightly touched Danny's shoulder as he passed by. It was a simple, friendly gesture and probably was not even noticed by Kenneth, but it touched Danny more deeply than just on his shoulder.

Danny felt a moment of cold panic when

he saw the mud wagon rolling in from the east. He recognized it. And the driver.

For an instant he thought the driver would surely recognize him, never mind that he had been wearing his flour-sack mask and was completely covered by a light duster.

Not that he was in any shape to run even if he was recognized. He still could barely move around the station with Kenneth or Anne lending an arm to lean on.

Danny sat tight in the rocking chair that was his usual daytime position and waited while the wagon pulled in and stopped.

Kenneth came out of the corral and removed his hat, using the back of his wrist to wipe his forehead. "Hey, Jim, how're you doing? Where's Tim? I thought he was with you the last time through."

The old man climbed wearily down from his perch on the driving box. "Tim is dead, Kenny. Shot by robbers after I left here the last time."

"Jesus, Jim. I'm sorry to hear that."

"I did everything I could for him, Kenny. Even thought he was going to make it. Then the gangrene set in. He died over in Garden City." The driver looked close to tears. He shook his head and moaned, "I don't know what I'm going to tell his mama. He was my oldest, you know. She wanted him kept close to home. Wanted him to go to clerking in a store. She . . . I'm the one wanted his company when I drive. Lettie was right. The fault was mine, Kenneth. I never should have insisted on him coming with me."

"The fault is with the sons of bitches that murdered him, Jim. Here now. You come inside. Let my Annie fix you something to eat. I'll tend your team for you." Kenneth hesitated a moment, then nodded toward the back of the mud wagon. "That box. Is that . . . ?"

"Yes, it is. They fixed him up nice in Garden City. Put a suit on him and everything. But, Lord God, I hope my woman won't insist on opening the box to see, him being dead so long by the time I get him home."

"Go inside, Jim." Kenneth raised his voice. "Annie? Anne! Come take care of Jim Carter here. He needs food and he needs praying over. Hurry up, Annie."

Carter stumbled blindly past Danny to get to the shelter of the relay station. He looked numbed by the loss of his son. His eldest, he had said. Dead now, killed by either Red or perhaps Henry.

Oh, Lord! Danny had never thought about the way their robberies might look to the person standing in front of their pistol muzzles.

Now this old man's life was shattered.

9

Eastern Colorado 1885
The temperature might not be freezing, but it was not far from it.

Danny removed his coat and shirt and carefully shook them out, trying to rid them of the dust and bits of broken grass stems that came from the hay he had been unloading. He wanted to get rid of as much as he could or they would itch him half to death when he put his clothes back on.

He pumped a bucket of frigid water and sopped a piece of rag in it, then used that to bathe himself as best he could. When he had wiped down everything he could reach, he turned the bucket up and dumped it over his head and upper body, shaking and shivering from the feel of it but at the same time invigorated.

He set the bucket aside and quickly dried off with a clean burlap sack, then put his shirt and coat back on.

Stepping into the station, he moved to the far end, beyond the long table, and stood for a moment soaking up the warmth that radiated from the potbelly stove there.

Kenneth and Will Tyler were drinking coffee at the table. Anne and baby Christopher — not only had Danny learned the kid was a boy, but over the past six months Danny had also learned to change a diaper — were at the back of the station, where Anne was preparing food.

"Come sit with us, Dan. There's something I'd like to discuss with you," Tyler invited.

"Sure, Will." Danny went first to the back of the room to pick up a cup and pour himself some steaming hot coffee, then joined the two men at the table. "What's on your mind?"

"You are."

Danny was puzzled. But not really worried. No one here knew anything about his previous activities. He had long since gotten over his fears that he might be recognized.

"Last time I was down to Trinidad I spoke to Don Colton about you," Tyler said.

"And he would be . . . ?"

"He's my boss. He's in charge of procurement for the company. Buying horses, grain and fodder or whatever else is needed. He's

110

the one buys the hay that I deliver here." Will smiled. "And that you've been busy unloading for me."

Danny waved the implied thanks aside.

"Kenneth said now that the weather is breaking, you intend to move along."

"Yes, sir. There's no job for me here. I know that. The place wouldn't support another man on the payroll, and I can't keep on being a drag on Kenny and Anne. I'm well enough to travel now, an' it's time that I do."

"You're no drag on this outfit," Kenneth was quick to put in. "You aren't afraid of hard work, Dan, and I'd be pleased as punch to have you stay here. But you're a young man and you're bound to have ambition. That's why I mentioned your situation to Will."

Tyler continued. "The thing is, Dan, if you'd like a job, Mr. Colton would be willing to take you on as an apprentice. The pay wouldn't be much, and the work would be hard, but it's honest labor."

Danny puffed his cheeks out and pursed his lips. Very slowly he exhaled. He had not expected anything like this.

"You come highly recommended," Tyler said with a smile. "By me and by Kenny both. Are you interested?"

"I . . . I don't know," Danny admitted. "You hit me pretty sudden here."

His intention — more or less — had been to get himself back on his feet and, now that it was springtime, head back to the Indian Nations to see if he could find the boys.

"I'd miss you, Dan. You're a big help to me. Which is exactly what I told Will to tell Mr. Colton. I'd miss you, but I don't want to hold you back."

"I don't know what to say, fellas. Truly I don't. But I sure can thank you. I never thought . . ."

"You don't have to decide right now. Take your time. If you want the job, you can ride back to Trinidad with me this trip or even the next time I come this way. If you want to come with me, though, I'll be driving back that way come morning."

Tyler grinned and slapped his leg. "For now, though, let's have one more cup of Annie's good coffee and then a big old bowl of her grass-rat stew."

"They aren't rats, dammit, Will. I told you they're prairie dogs," Kenneth returned. It was a long-standing joke between the two of them, and at first Danny had thought they were serious. They were not. In truth the meat was perfectly good grass-fed beef that was locally raised and butchered.

"Coming right up," Anne said from the stove. "No rats for you, Will. I put aside a mouse for your supper."

Ambition. What was it Kenny said? He was a young man and bound to have ambition. Except he honestly had not thought much about the future. Not until now. He and the boys went helling around the country taking what they wanted and living easy in between. No jobs. No worries. Well, not much in the way of worries. Maybe not enough.

But ambition? He hadn't really thought about the long haul. Had not thought about a job, a home, friends.

He liked the people he had come to know here at the station. Not just Kenny and Anne but the folks who passed through. It was a pleasure to visit with them in the evenings. It was even a pleasure to wear himself out with hard work and look forward to the reward of a hot meal and his cot in the tack shed.

Ambition. Interesting thought.

Danny finished dressing and walked out into the brittle cold of a clear dawn. He stood for a few moments drawing in deep breaths and looking slowly around. Then he strode across the yard and entered the big public room without knocking.

Anne was already at her stove. Kenneth and Tyler were seated at the table waiting for the first of the coffee to boil. All three looked up when he joined them.

"Well?"

"I'll be riding along with you today if the offer is still open, Will."

It did not take him long to pack. He had a spare shirt that some traveler left behind and that Anne washed and repaired for his use. He had the gunbelt and heavy Colt .45 that he had not strapped on in all the months he had been at the station. He had the clothing he was wearing the day he was injured. He had the contents of his pockets that day. It was not much.

He wrapped the gunbelt around his holster and shoved the resulting bundle into an empty grain sack, carefully folded the spare shirt . . . and he was packed and ready to travel.

Danny pulled his flat cap on — a cap instead of a wide-brimmed hat because it fit more readily under a flour-sack mask — and carried his meager bag of possessions out to the now empty hay wagon before entering the station.

"Ready when you are, Will."

"Right then. Help me hitch the team and we can get a start." He stood, knee joints cracking. "We'll shorten the hitch to four horses, though, and leave two here for Kenneth. We won't need six to pull an empty wagon."

Danny rather awkwardly sorted out the harness to build a four-horse hitch. Will Tyler watched but offered no criticism. It took a special knack to handle the big pulling horses and all the gear they required, and no one knew the ins and the outs of it to begin with. Danny would have to learn just as everyone else did, and that was sure to include making some mistakes along the way.

When the team was hitched and waiting, they went back indoors for a final cup of coffee before starting south.

Anne surprised Danny. A shy girl, she worked hard and said little. Now she approached Danny with a red scarf that she had spent the past week knitting in her spare moments. He knew it was intended for little Christopher, but now she handed it to him.

"To keep you warm," she said.

"I . . . I don't know . . ."

"You don't have to say anything, Daniel. Just know that we will miss you. And remember. This is your home now. It always will be." She gave him a brisk, hard hug, then turned and hurried away into the back room where she and Kenneth and the baby slept.

Kenneth offered his hand. "Annie said it, Dan. Come back anytime you can. I just wish we could keep you here."

"The gain is mine," Will said. He nudged Danny. "Come along, kid. You got work to do."

Danny began to grin. "Yes, *sir!*" He wrapped his fine new scarf tight around his throat and headed out the door into the dawn.

10

Southern Colorado 1885

Danny squirmed away from the moist heat of the girl's body. He did not mind swapping sweat when they were in the middle of things, but her body was hot and sticky and she had a stale smell. Next time maybe he should lift the skirts and sniff, find one who took a bath every now and then.

He pushed his legs out from under the blanket and sat up on the side of the narrow bed. He felt a light touch on his arm.

"Don't go, baby. Stay the night, eh? Half-price and you can spend the whole night. Do it all night long, eh."

"I got t' go. Got a load to haul tomorrow. Got t' be up early."

In the morning he would be taking a load out to Doan's station, then up to Batson's, then back in. He had seen the bill of lading. He would be carrying the usual assortment of necessities. Bacon, beans, rice, flour, lard and the like. It all had to be hauled to the relay stations.

Over the past several months, Danny had learned. He could build a satisfactory hitch now, large or short, and lately had been taken off the heavy haulers and given a light wagon and team of two well-mannered cobs to pull it. He knew the routes and the stations, and the company treated him well.

Danny slipped into his boots and buttoned his britches and picked up his brand-new wide-brimmed hat. There was a good reason for the larger brim, he had discovered. It kept the sun off the back of his neck and the rain out of his eyes. And it looked mighty fine too.

"You come back? See me again, Danny?"

"Sure, Carla. Sure thing." He said it but doubted that he would choose her again. Well, maybe. If she took a bath or bought some more of that sweet-smelling toilet water. He kind of liked that.

"Next time, Danny."

"You bet. Next time."

He left the crib and walked through the alley to avoid going back inside the noisy chaos in the Red Rooster. He'd had enough beer and carrying on for one night, especially when he had work to do come break of day.

Danny strolled back to his boardinghouse, enjoying the freshness of the night air. He stopped on the back porch to wash up, then let himself in through the kitchen, filching a chicken leg off the platter that was laid ready for breakfast.

"Hey! Watch that," Thelma, the landlady, warned. She did not mean it. Thelma liked to see her boys eat. She had eight boarders and treated each one as if he were her personal responsibility.

Danny winked at her and, munching the fried chicken, went upstairs to his room. Two dollars a week, meals included, but he had to take care of his own laundry if he wanted the sheets changed more often than monthly.

He undressed and lay down, relaxed and comfortable after his visit with Carla. He was eager to get on the road, eager to reach Doan's station.

Not that he cared anything about seeing Charles Doan again. Doan was a grouch and an opinionated asshole. But the man had a good-looking wife who had been flirting with Danny the last two times he was there. He had it in mind that she might be just about ready to slip out to the shed after her man went to sleep.

Yes, sir, he thought as he drifted toward

sleep, life wasn't bad.

"Out on your own are you, kid?" the company hostler commented when he led Danny's horses out.

"Yes, sir. First trip by myself."

Danny already had the harness sorted and laid ready. The hostler, Esau MacDonald, guided the first horse, the thick-bodied roan, into place and backed it toward the waiting doubletree. Danny deftly fitted the harness in place and buckled it on, then turned to the other horse, an old but steady brown, which MacDonald was already backing into position.

"Will Tyler says you're as good a helper as he's ever had. That's high praise."

"It's nice of him to lie like that," Danny said with a grin. "Will just doesn't want anybody to know how easy he is on his help. He's afraid folks will think he's soft."

"Laugh about it if you like, it's a nice compliment."

"Thanks for telling me, Mr. MacDonald."

The hostler grunted and helped Danny finish off the hitch. Danny climbed onto the box, shook out the lines and clucked to his team. He drove around to the loading dock and, carefully — he did not yet feel quite comfortable doing it — backed the wagon up to the dock.

Young muscles made short work of filling the bill of lading, then Danny returned to his — his very own, this trip — driving box.

He tipped his hat to the warehouse manager and, smiling, put his team into motion.

It was mid-afternoon by the time he finished unloading at Doan's. He dropped his freight off on the covered porch and left it there. The old fart could carry it inside himself.

Company policy said he had the right to bed and board while he was there, and Doan's young wife made it tempting to think about. He could see her peeping out at him every once in a while. Admiring the play of muscle in his arms, he suspected. But this was not the time. There was a coach due later, and Doan would only expect help if he stayed.

Besides, pretty she might be and with tits like bushel baskets — all right, in truth pecks not bushels — but Doan's woman could not cook worth a damn. Danny would cook for himself tonight and maybe stay over here on his way back in.

"You goin' south?" the old man asked.

"Ayuh. You know I am."

"Want you to take something down to Batson for me."

Danny was mildly surprised. This was the most conversation he had ever had with Doan. "I don't mind."

"Wait here. I won't be but a minute."

Doan went inside the station and emerged a moment later carrying an envelope. The paper was sealed with a drop of wax that had some sort of fancy figure pressed into it. Doan handed it to Danny and said, "For Batson. In person, mind. Nobody else." There was something in the man's voice . . .

Danny shrugged. It wasn't anything to him what Doan and Batson got up to.

He went around to the front of his rig and picked up the hitching weight he had clipped to the nigh horse's bit ring, then tossed the weight into the now considerably lighter wagon.

"I'll see you in a couple days," he said. But Doan had already turned away and was disappearing into his station building.

Danny spent the night on the road and arrived at Batson's in the forenoon of the following day. Batson, a sun- and wind-baked former cowhand, came out to greet him with a smile and a welcome.

"Coffee? My old lady just put some on fresh. Time I get these things unloaded it should be ready."

"I'd appreciate it, Sol, and if you don't mind the company, I'll stay over here tonight and rest these horses." Never mind that starting north early tomorrow would put him back at Doan's late enough that he would have an excuse to stay the night there . . . and maybe take that shot at Doan's pretty wife.

"Fine. Pull around close, and I'll unload."

"I can help you do that. Then I'll put the horses up. It won't hurt 'em any to stand hitched until everything is unloaded."

Company rules said Danny was responsible for loading and unloading — which he did not mind anyway — but Sol Batson was always willing to lend a hand. Unlike some people Danny could think of.

The two men made short work of the unloading, then Batson went inside to fetch out two cups of coffee while Danny drove the wagon over beside Batson's barn and unhitched the horses, draping the harness over the corral posts ready for use again in the morning.

This was dry country, with much sun and little rain, and harness or saddle leather dried out quickly. Danny reminded himself to soap the harness and oil it once he got back home to Trinidad.

Dry country, indeed. The truth was down

here at Batson's he was never quite sure if he was still in Colorado or had crossed over into New Mexico. Not that it mattered either way. He had long since quit worrying about whether there was any paper out on him. Maybe there still was, but those days were behind him now.

Danny hazed his pair of cobs into the corral, hung the bridles on a post beside the harness, and walked back to the station porch where Sol was waiting for him with coffee and the checkerboard. Batson did dearly love a game of checkers.

After supper — and two games of checkers, both of which Danny lost — they went back to the porch. The seating Sol provided on the porch for the comfort of the company's passengers consisted of empty kegs with pillows on top. Danny, and probably everyone else, would have preferred rocking chairs like Kenneth Copelane and most of the other station keepers had, but Sol claimed to prefer sitting on stools. Said it was better for a man's posture and therefore better for his lungs. Danny would rather have the rockers even if that were so.

"Tobaccy?" Sol offered as he filled his pipe and squinted down at the checkerboard.

"No, thanks. Not my vice."

Sol grinned. "How's about a drink then?"

"Now, that I could go for."

"Come along, Dan. I have a jug out in the shed. We'll see can we get rid of some of it."

Danny trailed his host across the yard to the weathered and haphazardly constructed toolshed. "I just remembered something," he said as Batson was fetching a jar of whiskey out of its hiding place in a tool chest. "Doan gave me something to carry to you. I almost forgot."

Danny pulled the slightly rumpled envelope from his back pocket and handed it to Sol.

"Thanks, Dan."

"Glad to help, Sol. Anytime."

Sol Batson twisted off the lid of the fruit jar filled with clear, colorless liquid and handed the jar to Danny. Fumes coming off the homemade whiskey were impossible to breathe, and the first swallow was so strong it made his eyes water.

Danny wiped his mouth, grinned and took another drink — smaller this time. "Good stuff," he said. "Thanks."

The country down here was almost flat. Endless miles of pale brown grass, interspersed with the occasional emerald green bottom where subsurface moisture collected. The day was fine — not too hot or too cold — and the team seemed to be feeling as good as Danny did. It was an easy pull with an empty wagon behind them.

Danny took a break in mid-afternoon. There was no rush to get back. In fact, he did not want to reach Doan's too early. He wanted a good excuse to stay the night there. With any kind of luck he could get Doan's woman in the hay pile. He would chat her up when she came out after supper to throw the scraps to her chickens. He just hoped there was no coach due through about then.

There was not one on the regular schedule, but schedules changed at the whim of horses, weather and breakdowns.

Still . . . with any kind of luck . . .

Danny clipped the hitch weight back onto the nigh horse's bit ring. He helped himself to a drink of tepid water from the small keg he carried under the wagon seat, then sat in the shade provided by the wagon box, leaning up against a wheel.

Down to the south he could see movement along the road to Batson's. Horsemen, he made out a few minutes later, shading his eyes and squinting to try to see a little better. Three . . . no, four horsemen. Moving fast too. Either they were local or they were loco, one or the other. That kind of speed was hard on an animal. He hoped they had good reason to be pushing their mounts so.

Twenty minutes later they were close enough for him to see the colors of their shirts. And the fact that all four of them were armed.

Not only were the men armed, they had their pistols in hand.

Shit! Danny grumbled to himself. He was about to be robbed. Not that he had so much on him as to be worth robbing. And not that he did not deserve it, considering that he had robbed so many himself in the past.

Still and all, it felt lousy to be on this end of a robbery.

He did not even have his revolver with him. It was back in his room in Trinidad. He had not touched it in months. Now that he needed it . . .

Danny stood and waited for the robbers to catch up with him.

He knew the deal.

Stand and deliver.

The riders stopped just short of running into him. Their horses tossed their heads, throwing slobber onto his shirt and huffing practically in his face. Danny's horses fidgeted and stamped, but this was no time to be worrying about that.

"I don't have much, but I ain't in a position to give you any trouble," Danny said. He began to turn his pockets out.

"What d'you think you're doing?"

"You're robbing me, ain't you?"

"Shit, no. We aren't gonna rob you," a bearded man in the middle said.

"We're gonna hang you, but we aren't gonna rob you," another put in. "We're Christian men. We'll give you time to write your folks if you got anybody to write to, and if you tell us your name we can put that on a marker for you."

"Hang me! What the hell for?"

"Rustling. As you damned well know."

"Mister, do you see any cows here?" He pointed to his wagon. "These horses an' an empty wagon. That's it."

"You know what you done. We caught you this time, you son of a bitch," one of them growled.

"I don't know what in hell you are talkin' about, but I don't have any cows. I've never had any cows. Short of eating it, I wouldn't know what to do with a cow if I was given one for a gift. So why are you accusing me of stealing cows?"

"You know why, damn you. You been supplying that bastard Batson with forged bills of sale. That's your end of it. Batson spilled everything."

Another of the men spat, "Before we hanged him."

One of them pulled a crumpled wad of paper from his jeans and waved it in front of Danny. "We found this on him. He told us where it came from."

"Sonuvabitch would've told us more but we hanged his lying ass first."

"He won't be stealing any more of our beef."

"And neither will you."

The four dismounted and began tying their tired mounts to the tailgate of the supply wagon.

If he had his pistol . . . but he didn't. Now that he needed it, the fool thing was still in the bottom of a burlap sack full of other stuff he kept but did not know why.

One of the men grabbed him by the arm and turned him half-around. "See this? Look. Look real close. Can you tell us you never seen it before?" He pushed the paper practically under Danny's nose. Another scrap of paper fluttered to the ground when he did so. That one Danny did indeed recognize.

"Look, dammit, you're making a mistake here," Danny protested, jerking his arm away from his accuser. "I see that envelope lying there. I gave it to Batson, all right, but I never knew what was in it. All I saw was the envelope. I recognize it by that wax seal. But I never — Another fellow asked me to carry it down to Batson. You say you *hanged* him?"

"Stretched the sonuvabitch's neck twicet as long as it used to was, by God."

"He shit his britches," another said. "It stunk something awful. I'm glad I'm not the one has to clean him up to bury him."

That got a laugh from the man's friends. Danny failed to find any humor in this.

"And now we're gonna stretch your neck too," someone said.

"Bob, unhitch those horses. There's no trees handy, so we'll hang him off the end of the wagon tongue."

They were serious about this, Danny thought. A chill ran up his spine, and he began to shake.

So this was what it was like. This was where he would die.

And this time, dammit, he was *innocent!*

Hang him. Dear God, they were going to hang him. And he did not even have a gun to defend himself.

Two of them collected the reins of all the horses and led them around to the back of the wagon. They dropped the tailgate and got busy tying the horses there.

A third cowboy walked to the front of the wagon. He unhooked the traces and hazed the cobs, still in harness, out away from the tongue.

The fourth, the bearded man who seemed to be the boss of the outfit, stood guard over Danny.

Hanged. Shot. Which would be worse?

Danny took a deep breath. Piss on this!

He jumped at the rancher. Grabbed the bastard's wrist with one hand and with the other snatched the man's Colt out of his holster.

He shoved the muzzle of the revolver hard against the underside of the man's jaw and cocked the hammer.

"All right now, dammit. Any one of you sons of bitches moves for a gun and there's gonna be brains an' blood flying all over the place." Danny clutched the man tight with

131

his free arm. If the guy got away from him, the others would be able to shoot. He jammed the pistol harder into the man's flesh. "Tell 'em."

All the fellow could get out was a gurgle. He had gone pale, and his knees were wobbly. No mystery there. Danny's knees felt mighty wobbly too.

"You. All three of you. Take off your gunbelts and hang them over your saddle horns. Do it now."

He was almost surprised that indeed they complied with exactly what he said.

But then when he and the boys were robbing people, they never had any trouble once folks saw they were under the guns. Well, almost never. Not until that one time when Danny got hurt, but that sort of did not count because he wasn't shot, he was run over by a wagon wheel.

Now these three were doing just what he said.

They kept looking at the bearded man — he had to be their boss — who by now was rising on tiptoe and looked about ready to break out bawling he was so scared. Likely frustrated too.

They quickly unbuckled their gunbelts and draped them over their saddles.

"That isn't good enough. Fasten those

buckles back again. I don't want anything slipping and falling. That would be real bad for this fella's health, if you know what I mean."

Danny had never in his life actually shot anyone. He hoped this would not be a first time.

"That's good. Now back away. Turn right around an' run over there. Go on now. Run. An' don't stop till I tell you to."

"Boss, what . . ."

"Do it, goddammit!" the boss croaked.

They turned and jogged away.

"Faster," Danny shouted.

The three cowboys picked up their speed just a little.

"Jeez," Danny moaned, "now what am I gonna do with you. I don't want t' shoot you. Honest I don't. But once I turn loose of you, I could be in trouble here, you know?"

"I won't . . . won't give you no trouble."

"I dunno, mister. Could be easier just to blow your brains out. Then I know you won't."

"No, I . . . I promise."

"Fat lot of good that does. But all right. I'm gonna let you step away. Go over there by the front of that wagon tongue. No fast moves though. I don't care how fast you

133

jump, you won't be faster than a bullet, and I'm a sure shot." That was a pure lie. Danny never had been particularly good with a gun. Not especially fast and not very accurate. He had only ever used one to intimidate. Thank goodness it seemed to be working again this time.

"Go on now. Over by the end of the tongue."

He glanced around. The team, still harnessed and trailing the lines on the ground, had wandered off in search of graze. They were perhaps fifty yards distant.

The three cowboys were now at least twice that far and moving slowly, heads down and likely tiring. The sons of bitches were not accustomed to going anywhere on their own feet.

All four saddle horses were patiently standing at the tailgate where they were tied. Fine!

Danny took his time. Keeping one eye on the bearded rancher and the other on what he was doing, he untied the horses one by one and carefully tied the reins of three of them to the tails of another until all four were tied together.

Then he swung into the saddle of the lead horse and began riding westward.

11

Indian Territory 1885

"Well, I'll be damned. Danny Southern. I haven't seen you in . . . What's it been now? A year or thereabouts. Come in. Come in here and have yourself a drink. On the house, lad."

"Hello, Cooter. You're right. It's been a long time."

The dark-hued storekeeper, a member of the Seminole tribe although he probably had no more Indian blood in him than Danny did, glanced toward the door. "Where's your partners, Danny? You boys are still riding together, aren't you?"

"We got, uh . . . We got separated, Cooter. That's what I'm doing here. Looking for them, I mean."

"Hell, kid, I haven't seen them since the last time I seen you."

"Damn. I was hoping t' find them around here."

Cooter shrugged. "Could be that they found somebody they like better. I'm sorry I can't help you though."

"That's all right. Listen, Cooter, are you still in, um, in business? You know what I mean."

"Still taking things in trade, sure. What do you have?"

"I've got three pretty decent horses, each of 'em with saddles. And I got two saddle carbines and a Remington revolver that I want to sell for cash money." He had swapped the other firearms along the way, exchanging them for food. The horses he kept until now. They wore brands, and Danny did not want anyone asking questions or looking for bills of sale. Cooter was not a man who asked about that sort of thing.

"Let me take a look, Danny. I'm sure we can come up with a price to make us both happy."

"We always could count on you, Cooter." Danny smiled. This was not home down in this country, but it was the closest thing to it that he had.

Danny dismounted and tied his horse to a post in the front yard. He took a narrow flagstone path to a little frame bungalow set amid a grove of sweet gum and dogwood. It was hard to get used to so much greenery after coming from the dry, brown West.

He stepped up onto the front porch and rapped lightly on the door. The man who answered it looked like a Methodist preacher, boiled collar and all. He wore spectacles and had a folded newspaper in one hand. He also wore his graying hair down past his shoulders.

"Hello, Mr. Dark Wing."

The Indian removed his spectacles and squinted, then he smiled. "Danny Southern. Nice to see you again, Danny. If you want the house back, though, I have to disappoint you. I have other tenants living there now."

"No, sir, I rode past there a little while ago and seen that you did. What I'm wondering is whether you know where I can find my friends. You know, the fellows I used to live with here."

Dark Wing shook his head. "I'm sorry, Danny. They never said where they were going. The two of them stayed here just a little while after you left them, then they pulled up stakes and rode away. They never said where they were going."

"Damn." Danny had been hoping he would find the boys still using this forgiving country as their headquarters. Now he did not know where to look.

"Is everything all right with you, Danny? You look upset."

"Oh, I'm okay, Mr. Dark Wing. Just a little . . . I don't know. Disappointed, I suppose you would say."

The Indian smiled. "One thing I'm sure will help. Come inside. My old woman is fixing a mess of hominy and side meat. There's more than enough for you to join us."

"Oh, I couldn't . . ."

"Nonsense. We'd enjoy the pleasure of your company."

"Well . . ." Danny smiled. "Thank you, sir. Just give me a minute to wash up an' I'll be right along."

"Another cup of coffee?"

"No, thanks. I'm full as a tick on a hound's ear." They were seated behind the house, beneath an open-sided thatched roof. A smudge was burning nearby to keep mosquitoes away. The smudge was not working, but then nothing really did.

"Then can I tempt you with a small cup of whiskey?" Dark Wing smiled. "Or two?"

"Maybe I'm not too full after all."

The old Indian pulled some split wood off the top of his woodpile and brought out a crockery jug. "Best sample it to make sure it hasn't gone bad," he said, pulling the cork and lifting the jug to his lips. He took a long draft, then passed the jug to Danny.

The liquor went down easy. "Soft as velvet," Danny said. "The man as made this is a craftsman."

Dark Wing nodded. "Thank you."

"You cooked this yourself? I never suspected."

The Indian shrugged. "It's illegal. Even here where they leave us alone about most things. For the white whiskey the deputies will come riding out from Little Rock. Break up a man's still and take away his living. Put him in jail for two, three years. I don't much like it known that I'm in the business."

"I can't say as I blame you," Danny said.

"Now, don't take this wrong, but when you and your friends were here I got the idea you boys were . . . well . . . not entirely on the up-and-up. If you know what I mean."

Danny pondered for a moment, then slowly and cautiously said, "I ain't actually admitting to anything, mind you. But I ain't arguing the point neither."

Dark Wing nodded. He too took his time before he spoke again. He took a drink from the jug. Pulled out a plug of tobacco and whittled off a small piece that he stuck in his cheek. Sat back in his wicker chair. Then he leaned forward.

"You seem to be at loose ends, Danny."

"Yes, sir, I expect that I am."

"You don't have a job nor a home to go to."

"No, sir, I don't."

"Well fixed for money, are you?"

Danny shook his head. "I got a few dollars in my pocket and no prospect for getting more. When that's gone, that's it."

"I thought as much." Dark Wing sat in silence a little longer. Danny waited for the old man to speak.

"Can you use that gun you're wearing?" he asked finally.

"Only passable well an' only if I have to. I've never shot anybody an' don't want to."

"You aren't some crazy hellion, Danny. That's one of the things I like about you. That plus the fact that you took the jug but drank from it in moderation. You like the whiskey but you aren't bound to it. That is important. And you can be trusted. I sense that about you too."

"Yes, sir?"

"As I've just admitted, I have a business to run here. One that isn't entirely legal,

140

you see."

"Yes, sir."

"The thing is, Danny, I need someone to make deliveries for me. Someone who has nerve but isn't eager to use it. There is some risk involved. I want you to know that right up front. The job pays passing well. Seventy-five dollars a month cash money and found. I'd throw in the use of a cabin I have down by Robbins Pond. Do you think you might be interested?"

Danny grinned. "Mr. Dark Wing, you just hired yourself a man."

The Indian leaned forward and extended his hand to seal the deal with a shake.

The cabin wasn't much — one room and an outhouse — but then Danny was not accustomed to comfort. There was a large pen for the horse and a stack of hay already in place. When he went inside he saw there was food, both canned and dry, on the shelves and wood by the stove. Dark Wing had it ready beforehand. Danny wasn't sure if that was a good sign or not.

Moving in consisted of carrying his saddlebags and bedroll inside and tossing them onto the little table in the center of the room.

He dragged the mattress outside and

emptied the straw out of it. Turned the ticking inside out to expose the seams and laid it in the sun. That should discourage any bedbugs left behind by whoever had this job before.

He burned the old straw and sat on a stool beneath the roof overhang at the front of the place to admire the view. There were trees. Lordy, but there were trees. Danny was not used to seeing so much green. He kind of liked it.

Robbins Pond was not all that much of a pond. Probably less than an acre. But it was a pretty enough thing, surrounded by cattails. Birds kept fluttering in and out of the cattails, and he could see some ducks paddling quietly on the far side of the pond.

There seemed to be no pump or well, but a platform of sturdy planks was built out over the near edge of the pond, extending past the cattails to open water, so he guessed he was supposed to draw his water there and carry it inside.

There was a bucket and washstand on the south side of the cabin and another bucket and ladle by the stove.

The kitchen consisted of a skillet, one pot and a mallet. Danny had no idea what the mallet was for. Whacking unwanted guests perhaps. Not that he expected many guests, wanted or otherwise.

All in all the place was more than good enough. Certainly better than he had been experiencing since those jaspers back in Colorado put him on the run again.

He supposed he was wanted back there now. Dammit. He'd had it good there. Had liked being able to live without looking over his shoulder all the time to see who might be coming after him. Now he was back on the dodge.

Still, things were looking up now that he would be working for Mr. Dark Wing.

Danny sat back, crossed his legs at the ankle and tipped his hat down over his eyes. He listened to the birds in the cattails and enjoyed the peace and quiet of Robbins Pond.

"Mules? Are you serious? Mules?"

Dark Wing smiled. "Don't look at me like that. I know what I'm doing. The tribal police aren't too curious, but you have to watch out for the federal deputies. That's why these mules. Old long-ears looks lazy, and everyone thinks they're slow. Not these boys. They can outrun most racehorses if they have to. The trick is not having to. Someone sees this rickety wagon being pulled by a pair of flea-bitten mules, they

143

don't generally suspect anything.

"You went to school, Danny. Did your teacher tell you the story of the Trojan Horse?"

"Sure. I remember that one."

"Well, think of this outfit as a sort of Trojan Horse. It isn't exactly what it seems. Now, look here and I'll show you what I mean." Dark Wing led Danny to the ugly contraption that passed for a wagon. It looked like it would fall to pieces if someone leaned against it.

"You have extra springs underneath, and these wheels are mismatched and ugly but they are strong and in good shape. Keep them that way."

"Yes, sir."

"The extra springs are because of this." Dark Wing lifted a section of floorboards in the wagon bed to reveal a space underneath. "Just the right size, you will find, to hold a standard gallon jug sitting upright. You can store a hundred eighteen gallons of product here and no one's the wiser. Look."

He let the floor back down. Picked up a handful of straw and dirt and scattered it in the bed. "Can you tell?"

Danny shook his head. "I'll be damned."

Dark Wing looked pleased with himself. "When you go out you'll carry a light load

144

in here for appearance' sake. Grain for the mules. Food for yourself. Nothing important, but if anyone looked in to see what you're hauling, all they will see will be those sacks and a cask of water, things like that."

"I like it," Danny said.

"Good. You can take your first load out tomorrow morning. I'll tell you where to go and who to see. You'll have to have a note showing who you are or the customers won't trust you. I'll give you that when you load the wagon. Now, come along. I want to show you where you pick the product up. It's a root cellar. But don't be going along the path to my still. Strangers aren't welcomed there and you are likely to be shot if you try to go there. Even if you are with me you could be shot. My people could think you are a deputy who has me in custody. Besides, there's no need for you to go there. Ever. Understood?"

"Yes, sir. I'm no more curious than I need to be."

"Good." Dark Wing smiled again. "I like you, Danny. I surely do."

"Easiest work I ever did," Danny muttered to himself as he hefted another pair of filled jugs into the back of the wagon. "Well, the second easiest anyhow."

The truth was, robbing folks was easier. More exciting too. Still and all . . .

It occurred to him to wonder which drew the longer prison sentence, armed robbery or moonshining. He didn't know. Was reluctant to ask anyone too.

His back was beginning to ache from the unaccustomed bending and lifting repeated over and over again. One hundred eighteen jugs. That meant . . . it took him a moment to cipher it out . . . fifty-nine times he had to bend and lift to fully load the wagon.

When he was done, Danny set the false floor back in place over the whiskey and loaded his phony cargo of grain and canned goods. He threw some hay into the stall where his saddle horse would stay during the day and made sure there was fresh water in there too. Then he slapped his hands and britches to shake off the loose straw chaff he had collected and went to fetch the mules.

The harness was straightforward, pretty much what he was already used to except for the crupper straps to compensate for the mules' narrow flanks. It took little time for him to harness and hitch the lanky, lazy, flea-bitten beasts. Finally he led the team and wagon out, carefully pulled the barn doors closed and climbed rather gratefully onto the driving box.

"Hyah! Hyup, boys, hyah." Danny gave the driving lines a shake and his pair set off at a brisk walk, their heads bobbing and long ears flopping.

It occurred to him again to wonder about those prison terms. Not that he expected trouble. But then a fellow never knows what lies ahead.

12

Northern Indian Territory 1886

"Thanks for helping me, George." Danny set the last two jugs down and got busy replacing the false floor in the wagon while George Hanson arranged the newly delivered whiskey in the pit concealed within his barn. Hanson was one of the customers Danny particularly liked.

The man climbed out of the pit, covered it with planks, a bit of dirt and a small pile of straw, then stood and brushed himself off. "Come inside, Danny. I have your money set aside ready. Would you like a drink or maybe something to eat?"

"No liquor. I don't much have the taste for it anymore, but I could stand a beer and a bite to eat."

"You'll have to make do with coffee or tea. Beer is too bulky. Hard to hide from the tribal police. Or those son of a bitch federals. Pushy bastards. They got no respect for a man's rights."

All of Danny's customers despised the federal deputies. George Hanson more than most.

"Coffee would be fine, George, thanks."

Danny pulled his wagon out of the barn and took it around to the front of the little store. He got down from the box and clipped the tether of a hitch weight to the bit of his near mule. He took a moment to scratch the animal behind its long, floppy ears, then went inside Hanson's store.

George's Indian wife, Beatrice, was behind the counter. A family of three, all of them Indians to judge by appearance, were browsing the shelves of goods the Hansons had to offer.

"The boy here is hungry, woman. What do we have?"

Beatrice smiled. She was a homely woman but gentle and kind. Smart too. She could calculate price totals in her head quicker than Danny could figure them on paper. "Hello, Daniel. Would you like some meat? We have a fresh-killed antelope hanging in the shed."

"Don't bother with that. Some jerky and a couple pickled eggs and I'm fine," he said.

"It is no bother, Daniel. Let me make you a nice lunch."

"Thank you, Miz Hanson. That's mighty nice of you." Danny removed his hat and sat at one of the two tables provided in an open area at the side of the store building. George brought a pair of steaming cups and joined Danny there.

"That coffee smells good."

"Fresh-boiled."

Danny lifted the cup to his lips, but before he could drink he heard a brief scuffle and then a yelp of pain from the other end of the store.

"Bastard," George mumbled.

"Who d'you mean?" Danny asked, craning his neck to see what was going on. His view was blocked by the tables of goods in the middle of the store.

"Matthew Swift Runner is his name. He's a real asshole." There was another cry of pain from that end of the room. "I can't say anything to him because I'm white, and Swift Runner has a lot of influence around here. If I got into a squabble with him I might as well burn the place and walk away, for I surely couldn't make a living." The sound of muted thumping and banging could be heard now. "But he's like that all the time."

Danny could hear a kid's voice saying something — obviously pleading — in a language he did not understand. Then there was more thumping.

"Excuse me for a minute, George." Danny set his coffee aside and stood. He could see now that Swift Runner was alternately taking a strap to a boy of eight or so and punching a slender, moon-faced Indian woman. The boy was pleading for his mother, not for himself, Danny noticed.

Danny's expression was grim, and there was no humor in the hint of smile that tugged at his lips. He hitched up his britches and headed for the other end of the store.

Swift Runner backhanded the boy across the face. The kid flew backward, lost his balance and crashed into Danny's legs as Danny approached the threesome. That seemed to infuriate Swift Runner all the more. He shouted at the boy and tried to kick him. The shoe missed but only by inches.

"Whoa up, mister," Danny said. "There's no need for something like that. He didn't mean t' do it."

"Not you business, you son bitch." Swift Runner kicked at the boy again, and this time the toe of his shoe connected with the kid's hip. The mother screamed something and tried to get between Swift Runner and the boy.

Her diversion worked. Swift Runner turned his attention to the mother and punched her in the face.

"That's enough," Danny growled.

"Get out or I hit you, son bitch."

"Y'know," Danny said, smiling, "that's twice now you've made the mistake o' calling me that."

He stepped forward toe-to-toe with Swift Runner and stared him in the face. The man was no taller than Danny, but he had a blocky build and a broad face, with the high cheekbones of his people. He had long black hair held in a thick braid down his back.

"Son bitch," Swift Runner snarled. The man's breath was foul.

Danny threw an underhand punch, knuckles forward blade-like instead of formed into a fist. He hit Swift Runner in the breadbasket just as hard as he could manage.

Swift Runner doubled over, gasping for air. He staggered back, turned around and threw up onto a pile of new overalls. When he turned around again, Danny was waiting for him with a solid right hand that landed flush in the middle of Swift Runner's face. Cartilage snapped and blood began coursing down the man's chin and neck and soaking his shirt.

Danny hit him again, with a clubbed fist that broke Swift Runner's jaw and put him on the floor.

Danny drew back his foot with the intention of putting the boot to Swift Runner, but there would have been little point to it. Swift Runner was out cold.

"I'll be damned," Danny said to George Hanson, who had come up behind him. "I didn't know I could do that." He looked at his fist, obviously pleased with himself.

"Do you want a suggestion?" Hanson asked.

"Sure, George. What's that?"

"Get out of here before he wakes up. He's one mean bastard, and he wouldn't be above shooting you. You'd have to kill him to stop him. Not that there'd be anything wrong with that, but a white man who kills an Indian, never mind justification, he's going to have a hard time with the tribal police. It'd be best if you leave."

"Without my dinner?"

"I'll give you something to carry with you."

"Whatever you say. It's annoying though."

"That may be, but it's sensible. Now go on. Git."

Danny went back to the table for his hat and a swallow of coffee. He headed for the door. The Indian woman and boy were standing there waiting for him. They followed him outside and climbed onto his wagon, the woman getting on the seat in front and the boy sitting in back on a sack of grain.

"Where're they going?" he asked Hanson.

"With you."

"The hell you say."

"Danny, Swift Runner might well kill them if they stay here. Take them along for now. You can dump them someplace later on, but for now let them get out of that prick's reach."

"Yeah, I guess that won't hurt anything." Danny sighed and shrugged. He climbed onto the seat beside the woman and gathered up the leathers.

"So, uh, what's your name?"

She smiled and said something back in a tongue that did not much sound like the Cherokee and Seminole languages that he did not understand but at least was accustomed to hearing around Aaron Dark Wing.

"Do you speak any English at all?"

"Englis', yes." She pointed to Danny. "Yes. Engli'."

He tried again. "What's your name?"

The smile faded, and she launched into a long and totally incomprehensible account of . . . he knew not what. Then the boy stood up behind the seat, clinging to it with his head between the two adults, and he got into the conversation. But not a word of it in English.

Danny shut up and concentrated on driving.

Danny finished unloading the last jugs from the wagon. Immediately the woman and the boy jumped in to replace the false bottom and the sacks of phony cargo. While they were busy doing that, Danny turned to the Osage merchant this delivery had gone to. The storekeeper was counting out payment for his whiskey. Danny accepted that and dropped it into the bull scrotum pouch that was reserved for Dark Wing's money, then said, "Jim, I need your help with something."

"Sure, Dan. What you want?"

"This woman here. Can you talk to her?"

Jim Otter gave him a quizzical look.

"I mean, do you and her have the same language? Can you understand what she's saying?"

"I don' know, Dan. I see." Otter turned to the woman and spoke to her, hesitated and tried again. The woman returned something, and the two of them went back and forth for a minute or so.

Otter turned to Danny and said, "She is Kiowa. One of the wild tribes. She sent away, she and that boy."

"What are their names, Jim?" He waited a little longer while Otter and the woman talked.

"Her name, I do not have words for it," Otter said at length. "You know the soft feel of wind before a summer rain? That is her name. The boy, he does not have a real name yet. He is not old enough to choose. You call them what you want."

"Okay, then she's Windy and the boy is . . . I dunno . . . Henry. I used to have a buddy named Henry. It's a good name."

Otter turned back to the woman and boy and spoke with them, repeating their new names several times. Each struggled a little with the sounds but got them out after a few attempts.

Windy and Jim Otter talked a little more, then Otter told Danny, "She is proud to belong to such a brave warrior."

Danny's brow furrowed in puzzlement. "That asshole Swift Runner?"

"No, you idiot. She belongs to you now. She is your woman. Will keep your lodge.

Cook your meal. Warm your bed. The boy, he will carry the wood for you. Bring in water. Feed these mules. Anything you say. They both belong to you."

Danny was flummoxed. "Jim, I don't need . . . I mean I didn't fight to take her away from that bastard. I just wanted to help out."

"Well, you have her now. She will be good to you. She hope you will not beat her much."

"I . . . Lordy, I don't have words."

"No matter," Otter said, apparently thinking Danny meant the language gap. "She belongs to you now. Show her what you want one time. After that, point. She will do."

"I'll be damned," Danny muttered.

He took a fresh, hard look at Windy. She had a round face. But she might not be so ugly once the purple bruising and the lumpy swelling subsided from her many encounters with Swift Runner's fists and feet.

Be damned, he thought.

With a shrug he climbed back onto the wagon and motioned for Windy and Henry to join him. "I'll see you next trip, Jim. Thanks for your help."

Danny shook out the lines and set his mules into a walk. He was looking forward to getting home this evening.

But what in *hell* was he going to do with Windy and Henry?

Danny put the mules up with a scratch behind the ears for each of them — darned if he hadn't come to like the ugly creatures — and gave his horse a scratch beneath the jaw by way of a hello. He threw hay into the corral and drew a tarp over the fake cargo in the wagon bed so it would not start to look as moth-eaten and phony as it was.

Windy and Henry stood mutely watching his movements, then followed him to the cabin. When Danny picked up the bucket and headed toward the pond, the woman stopped him, jabbering away about something that he could not comprehend.

She took hold of his wrist with one hand and the rope bale of the bucket with the other, tugging gently until he gave in and let her have the bucket.

"What are you . . ." He stopped. It was pointless to talk to her. He shrugged his shoulders and held both palms upward in inquiry.

Windy bobbed her head and said something. She handed the bucket to the boy and motioned him toward the pond, then she pointed to the bucket and next to the boy.

"I . . . uh . . . you mean it's his job now, eh?"

She responded with a smile, then shooed the boy on his way.

Danny led the way inside again and went to the stove, intending to start a fire for supper. Windy observed, then gently pushed in front of him, clearly taking over the cooking duties.

Later, after a meal of corn cakes and bacon, after Windy and the boy did the washing up, after the boy refilled the wood bin and Windy set a batch of dough ready for the morning, Danny had an idea of what some Eastern pasha must feel like, being waited on hand and foot. He watched the two of them for a while, then went outside to sit under the roof overhang with his feet propped on a block of wood and his arms crossed over a full belly.

He checked on the horses and visited the outhouse as the night sounds began. When he went back inside, a lamp was burning on the table. A pallet had been laid on the floor against the wall opposite his bed.

Windy said something to the boy, who dutifully went to the pallet, stripped off his clothes and crawled under the blanket. She then tapped Danny on the chest and pointed to the bed, stationing herself beside the lamp. When he did not move, she insistently motioned him to bed.

With a shrug he kicked off his boots and removed his shirt and trousers. He normally found it more comfortable to sleep naked, but he hesitated now, getting into bed still wearing his smallclothes.

The woman knelt and tucked Henry in for the night, speaking to him softly in the glow of the lamp. The kid smiled and squeezed his mother's hand and she sang to him. A lullaby, Danny supposed. He wished he understood the words.

She smoothed the boy's hair back and said something more to him, then came to the table and leaned over to direct a puff of air down the lamp chimney, sending the room into darkness.

Danny closed his eyes and prepared to sleep.

He came fully awake again a moment later when he felt the woman's presence beside his bed. For one ugly moment he felt a flush of alarm. If she wanted to harm him . . .

He felt his blanket being pulled back. Felt Windy's weight on the bed. Felt her warmth. Felt her flesh envelop his.

He was smiling when finally he fell asleep

with the woman tucked tight against his side.

"I see you finally took a woman for yourself." Dark Wing laughed. "It's about damn time. Young, strong fella like you needs a woman to keep him warm at night."

"You 'see'? How could you see anything about me. You haven't been around that place in all the time I've been living there."

Dark Wing snorted. "I know more than you might think. I have friends. That's one of the blessings I've learned to treasure in my old age."

"Old! You? You ain't never gonna get old. But I still don't see how you found out about Windy so quick."

"Windy? That's a terrible name for a woman even if she is from one of the wild tribes. What about the boy? What's his name?"

"I call him Henry after a friend I used t' have."

"Nice that you honor him by naming the boy that," Dark Wing said. "Would you mind if I come visit sometime? I would like to really 'see' this woman you call Windy."

Danny finished filling the wagon bed with whiskey, then put the floor and fake cargo in place on top of it. He tossed the hitching weight into the driving box and led the patient mules outside while Dark Wing covered the storage pit.

He climbed onto the seat and touched the brim of his hat to Dark Wing, who had become as much friend as he was employer. "I'll be back tomorrow evening. If you happen to go by the cabin, tell Windy that, would you please? I doubt she understood much of anything I was trying t' tell her this morning, about being gone overnight and all."

"Excellent," Dark Wing exclaimed. "Now I have a duty to go by and meet this wild woman of yours. Have a good trip, Danny. Stay away from the tribal police."

Danny clucked to the mules and braced himself against the slight jerk forward as they leaned into the traces.

He was kind of looking forward to getting home the next evening, and not just because he would be able to sleep under a roof instead of under a tarp in the back of the wagon. Danny was smiling as he pulled into the yard.

His smile faded. There was no sign of Windy or the boy. Smoke trickled out of the chimney, but that could have been from a fire left untended for hours.

It surprised him how disappointed he was that they had gone. Not that he could blame them for wanting the freedom to go wherever they pleased.

He wondered if Dark Wing had had a chance to speak with them. If he had, he might be able to offer an explanation. Or at the least a good-bye.

Sighing, Danny drove to the pen and parked the wagon. He unhitched, led the mules inside and stripped the harness from them, then took his time about sorting and hanging the harness leather. He was in no hurry to go inside to an empty cabin.

Eventually he ran out of chores to do outside and headed for the cabin. He was tired and he was hungry and all of a sudden he was peeved to find that the woman and kid had flown without so much as a thank-you.

When he opened the door and stepped inside, he walked into a different place from the one he'd left the previous morning.

The whole house had a warm and comforting aroma. A stew was bubbling on the stove. The boy was sitting on the edge of his cot grinning at Danny. Danny's bed was tidy, covered with a new blanket. A brace of rabbit carcasses hung from the rafter poles near the stove. And Windy stood waiting for him with a cup of whiskey.

"How . . . where . . . ?"

Both Windy and Henry were grinning hugely. The boy jumped up from his cot — it occurred to Danny that there hadn't *been* a cot before; probably Dark Wing brought it — and ran to proudly show Danny some scraps of cord.

It took Danny a moment to recognize what it was that Henry was so proud of. Snares. The kid had made snares out of some scrap cord. He was the hunter who provided the rabbits. Which suggested that the stew that smelled so good was rabbit meat along with . . . God knew what.

Danny went to the stove and used a wooden paddle — where had that come from — to stir the contents. Chunks of rabbit. Thick gravy. Spuds. And some roots that Danny did not recognize. Those must have come from the woods around the pond.

"Damn!" he muttered. Then he smiled.

Yeah. This was all right. This was nice to come home to.

He beckoned the boy to him and gave the kid's shoulder a squeeze, then hugged Windy close.

This was almost like having a family, by damn.

Danny cut down a pair of young saplings. They were too short, too thick at the butt and too weak at the tips, but they would do.

He pulled ten feet or so of twine off a ball of the stuff and rubbed it with boot polish to darken it, then tied that to the tips of his poles. He broke some dead twigs off the bottom of a nearby fir and tied those onto his cord a few feet from the end.

The boy watched his every move, the kid's dark eyes darting.

"Now the best part," Danny said as he tied the hooks onto the end of the lines.

He picked up the cracked and discarded canning jar full of dirt, full too of worms he and Henry had dug earlier, and carried it all down to the pond.

"Now let's catch us some supper for your mama to cook," he said, sitting down on the edge of the little dock with his bare feet dangling in the water. Damn, he hadn't done that since he was a kid himself.

The boy watched intently as Danny dug his fingers into the loam in the jar and extracted a worm to thread onto his hook.

Danny tossed his baited hook onto the quiet surface of the pond. The dry twig acted as a bobber quite as well as cork would have.

"Now you," he said, handing the second makeshift pole to Henry.

The boy's grin was huge as he too probed the jar of dirt for a fat, juicy worm.

"Care for a little more somethin' to eat?" the squat, dark man offered.

"No, thanks, Walter. I'm as full as a tick." Danny rubbed his belly, which was indeed full of fatback and hominy.

"Then how's about some corn?" Walter Two Birds nodded toward one of the jugs Danny had delivered that morning. "It's good for the digestion, they tell me."

Danny laughed. "That may be so, but unlike you I got work t' do this afternoon."

"I work. Beat my women much if they don't do what they ought."

Danny never had quite worked out whether Walter considered all three of his women to be wives or if two of them were employees. Not that it mattered. The man paid cash for his whiskey and always had a smile and a meal to offer.

"You hear the rumors, Danny?"

"That kinda depends, Walter. What rumors are you talkin' about?"

"Tribal council, they say, is getting pissed

166

that so much whiskey is being sold. Federal deputies come. Make much noise. Demand this, demand that. Tribal council is gonna crack down on you. You be careful, Danny. Tell Aaron what I say. Might be time for you to lay low."

"I'll tell him, Walter, and thank you."

If there were rumors about, it was almost certain that Aaron Dark Wing would already have heard them. But Danny would pass the message along anyway, just to be sure.

One of Walter's pack of black-haired, bright-eyed kids came running out of the cabin. Danny never had gotten it quite straight which of the children belonged to which of the women. Or if all were Walter's. The kid — this one seemed to be a girl, although even that could have been in question — excitedly spouted something in Cherokee. Danny did not have to understand the language to understand the message: "Come quick, Mama needs you."

Walter sighed and stood. "Excuse me, eh."

"You go on. I have t' put some more miles behind me anyway, so I'd best be moving. Thanks for the dinner, Walter."

"See you next trip, Danny."

"Aye. Next trip."

Danny hadn't even gotten his driving lines

sorted before he was thinking about getting home.

"Hewoe, Da'nee." Windy was grinning hugely, obviously proud of herself about something. It took Danny a moment or two to realize that she had just greeted him. In English. Sort of.

He grabbed her up, laughing, and hugged her until he became afraid that he might hurt her ribs.

He kissed her. Apparently that shocked Windy almost as much as it did him. In all the time they had been living together he had never kissed her. He had taken her body, but this was the first time he had kissed her. He hadn't planned to. It just happened. It felt right when he did it too, he marveled.

So he kissed her again.

"Hewoe, Da'nee," she repeated, smiling.

Danny hugged her hard and ruffled Henry's hair.

It was good to be home.

"Let me ask you something," Danny said to Aaron Dark Wing as he loaded whiskey jugs into the wagon. "If a fella wanted to live permanent with one woman . . . like if he wanted to get, well, married . . . I mean, how do folks around here take to that? If the woman is Indian, that is, and the man is white?"

Dark Wing chuckled. "Any particular woman you have in mind, Danny?"

"Well, sure. What the hell d'you think I am?"

"I don't want to discourage you, son, but assuming it's Soft Breeze you're thinking about . . ."

"Soft Breeze? Who the hell is Soft Breeze?"

"That's a lot closer to her name than Windy, boy. Now, if I may continue, if it's Soft Breeze you're thinking about, there isn't no need for you to do anything permanent like marrying her. She belongs to you. She's yours for as long as you want her, and when you're done with her you can walk away with no regrets and no obligations."

"But I . . ."

"I know. That isn't the way things are done in your world. 'Tis in hers." Dark Wing reached into a pocket and pulled out his pipe. "She does like you, by the way. She tries hard to please you. She's trying to learn how to speak English so she can please you better. But you got to know that she still belongs to the wild tribes."

"What's that supposed to mean?"

"I mean her ways are more different than

you might think. She worries that you don't care anything about her."

"But I . . ."

"You never beat her. By her lights that must mean you don't care enough to care what she does."

"Jesus, Aaron. D'you mean to tell me she'd be happier if I was to beat her next time I come home?"

The Indian nodded. "It would prove that you care about her."

Danny shook his head and groaned. "Crazy damn people, you Injuns."

"I'm serious, Danny. Try it. You wouldn't have to beat her hard. Just a little. Like a spanking for grown-ups."

"I'll think about it," Danny said. But he knew he would not.

Danny climbed into the wagon, and Dark Wing swung the barn doors open so he could drive out on his delivery rounds.

"Have a safe trip."

Danny touched the brim of his hat and clucked to the mules.

13

Southern Kansas 1886

"I'm surprised to see you, Dan."

Danny looked down at the bearded store-keeper and raised an eyebrow. "Now, why would that be, Cletus? You know I make my rounds regular. This is your week." He grinned. "Or did you lose track o' the time?"

"I'm s'prised because there's trouble. Figured you'd either be running by now or else in jail. How long you been out, anyway?"

"Three nights. This is the end of this route. I don't know about no trouble."

"Reckon you're lucky then. The damned federals been pushing the tribal police to clean up the illegal whiskey trade, so the police finally got off their red asses and started arresting folks. Dark Wing is in jail. I hear they've confiscated all his property and are holding him without bond.

"All the people that work the stills are

either in jail or in hiding. Same with about half of us that buy from him. The boy that brought the news to me said you was likely in jail too. There's an arrest warrant out on you for sure."

"Can they do that?" Danny asked. "The tribal police, I mean. Can they arrest a white man?"

"I don't know that much about it, but I'm for damn sure the federal deputies have that authority. I suppose the Injun police could take you in on their behalf." Cletus Jones shook his head and added, "Anyhow I wouldn't test their authority if I was you. Best you don't show yourself back there, Dan. Not if you want to keep looking at jail cells from the outside in."

"Damn!" Danny grumbled.

With a sigh he climbed down from the wagon and stood there for a moment trying to think this through. Finally he looked up. "I have ten jugs aboard, Cletus. D'you still want them? They'll be my last delivery, mind. I can't tell you if there will be any more coming. Ever."

"I'll take them, Dan. Pull around back and unload them like usual."

"Fine. And would it be all right if I stay the night here? I got some serious thinking to do."

"Yes, certainly. Put your mules in the pen yonder and come inside. I'll see you don't go hungry."

Danny nodded, but his thoughts were distant and unfocused. He felt sick to his stomach. Gone. It was all gone.

Shit!

What was he supposed to do now? Everything he owned was back by Robbins Pond at the cabin that Aaron Dark Wing let him use. His savings. His clothing. Windy. Most of all Windy. And the boy. He did not love them, exactly, but he was comfortable with them. They were his family. Yet if he went back to claim them, he would be imprisoned.

He could not even claim he hadn't done the crime. He had. He'd broken the law every day since he first met Aaron. Now that was all coming crashing down on top of him.

Danny lay in the dark on the pallet Cletus Jones had laid out for him and tried to take stock.

He had the two mules and a wagon that was in a lot better shape than it appeared. He had the clothes on his back, the five dollars he had left home with and a pouch with two hundred thirty-six dollars that he had been paid for the whiskey he delivered this

173

time out. He had a good revolver and rifle and the beans and other foods sitting in the back of the wagon as decoy goods in case he was stopped and questioned.

He also had arrest warrants outstanding in Colorado and Indian Territory and quite possibly here in Kansas too, although those might well have expired or at least been forgotten.

What he had was really damned little in the way of prospects.

Danny lay there, eyes wide open, listening to the pop and crack of Cletus's stove cooling down until the small hours of the night before he finally fell asleep. He still had no idea what he would — or what he could — do next.

"Where're you bound, Dan? Not back to Aaron's place, surely."

Danny finished buckling the harness straps and patted the mules' dry, dusty necks. He stepped back, looked at Cletus and shrugged. "Away from here. I think . . . I think I'm gonna go home, Cletus. It's been a long time, and I don't much care for being alone in the world. That is something I learned just recent. I'm a man as likes family. Reckon I'll go back to mine."

"I wish you luck, Dan."

Danny extended his hand to the man. "Thank you, Cletus. I'm grateful more than you could know."

"Good luck to you, son."

Danny climbed onto the box, took up the lines and clucked to his mules.

It took four days of steady travel to get there. Not that he had any reason to hurry, and he was used to sleeping on the road and making do on his own.

He did have to stop to buy food. His first day out away from familiar surroundings he'd intended to cook a mess of the beans he had been hauling around for months at a time, but they were infested with weevils. He dumped the entire sack on the roadside. If there were any birds or small animals that wanted the wormy things, they were welcome to the meal.

When he reached the outskirts of town, he felt the same stomach-clenching flutter of nervous excitement that he always had when he and the boys were going to pull a robbery.

Surely no one would remember him or connect him with those long-ago local robberies. That was possible but unlikely. The nervousness came from anticipating seeing his mother again. Would she still be living with that man? Would she even want to see her son again?

It was worrisome.

Danny drove first to the livery. There was a boy busy cleaning the stalls. Probably he was some kid who had been in the primary grades when Danny graduated from high school here. "Yes, sir, what do you need?" the boy asked.

"I'm looking for Jim Cooley. Is he still around?"

"In there." The barn helper — oh, Danny well remembered what that job was like, and at this same stable too — pointed to the tack room where Cooley had his bunk.

"Thanks." Danny climbed down and clipped the hitch weight to the near mule's bit, then entered the barn. The smells of hay and manure and horseflesh brought memories racing back. Most of those memories were good ones. Better than he might have thought. Better than he probably had any right to. It had been good being a kid here. He wondered what had gone wrong to bring him to this point, homeless and on the run. He'd hardly noticed it happening at the time. Now . . .

"Hello, Mr. Cooley."

The old man was stretched out on his cot. He had a newspaper lying on his chest but was not reading it. He sat up when Danny spoke to him.

"Do I know you?"

"You used to. Me and Red Clybourne and Henry Read. We all used t' run together. Used to rent horses from you sometimes."

Cooley rubbed his eyes. They were moist and seemed cloudy. Danny guessed he could no longer see very well. After a few moments he said, "Yeah. Now I remember. You're Miz Southern's boy. What's your name again?"

"Daniel. Dan. Southern. You're right about that. I've . . . I've come home."

"Where's the other two?"

"We split up a while back. I'm by myself now."

"You gonna be wanting to take out horses at night like you done before?"

"No, sir, that isn't what I came about. I, uh, got two really good mules and a wagon out here. I won't be needing them anymore, and I'd like to sell them. You still buy stock, don't you? And the wagon?"

"Let me take a look at them." Cooley stood, his knee joints popping.

"They're good mules."

"Everybody's mules is good mules," Cooley returned, "leastways to hear them tell it."

"Yeah, but these really are good mules. It's just that I don't need them anymore. I'll be settling down now."

Danny heard the words come almost unbidden from his mouth and he knew that it was true. The time had indeed come for him to quit his rowdy ways and make something of himself. He had not consciously decided that, but he supposed that somewhere deep inside he had known it all along. It was time now for him to steady down and start living a decent life.

Danny took the money and stuffed it into his pocket. He was about half pleased and the other half pissed. The wagon and team were worth at least two hundred dollars, and Cooley knew it, but fifty dollars was the best Danny could get out of him. Still, it was fifty dollars more than he'd had when he drove in here.

"Be all right if I leave my stuff here until I decide where I'm gonna be staying?" he asked.

Cooley nodded. "Fine with me, but I ain't responsible for it. I won't be watching over it."

Which probably suggested that Cooley himself would go through Danny's things to see if there was anything he wanted to pilfer.

Not that there was anything of value. Just the rifle, food and a few articles of clothing. He hadn't exactly had time to pack.

"I'll be back directly," Danny said.

He left the livery barn and headed down the street.

Home. It looked good to him. There were . . . he counted . . . two new structures since he and the boys left. Rogers had painted the front of his store. Green with white trim. It looked nice.

There wasn't much activity on the street. A couple wagons. A handful of pedestrians. That was it.

Danny recognized almost everyone he saw. Even the coonhound that lay curled on a cocoa mat in front of the Grange Hall. It or one just like it had been there when he and the boys left town.

For some reason he was reluctant to go see his mother. He was actually a little bit shaky now that he was here.

He delayed the moment by turning in at the saloon where they used to sneak in the back door and steal whiskey. The man behind the bar was new to town since Danny lived there.

"What will it be, neighbor?"

"Beer and a shot, please." He dug into his pocket and brought out some change, picked a quarter out of it and laid it on the bar. He wanted the beer to take care of his thirst and the shot to help settle his nerves. Damn if he knew why he felt so jumpy.

The bartender delivered his drinks. Danny took a swallow of the beer, then quickly downed the shot. He could feel it warm in his belly.

"Another?"

Danny shook his head. There was a temptation to have another and a host of others after that one, but . . . no. He needed to be sober when he went to see his mother again. He settled for the beer and a handful of salty pretzels.

The beer only lasted for so long though.

It was time.

Danny took a deep breath, put a smile on his face and opened the front door.

"Ma? I'm home. Home to stay."

He heard footsteps in the kitchen and the clang of a pot being set onto the stove. A moment later a middle-aged woman appeared in the doorway. "Who are you?"

"I . . . Who are *you?*"

"I'm Gladys Rowe, and what are you doing in my home?" She looked like she was ready to hit him or throw something if he didn't speak up soon.

"I'm . . . This is my mom's house. Or . . . used to be."

"Oh." Gladys Rowe sniffed her disapproval. "Her. Her and that Gypsy of hers left. Left owing money to half the town the way I hear it. Not that I'm saying anything, no, sir, not me." Gladys Rowe scowled.

"I . . . Jesus." Danny turned tail and hurried out of Gladys Rowe's front room.

It was Danny's firm intention to get drunk. Gut-twisting, puke-spewing, falling-down drunk.

He headed back the way he had just come, away from the house where he'd grown up and toward the saloon where they had the medicine that would mute his pain.

He would have himself a good drunk and then . . . He had no idea what he would do after that. He would worry about that when the time came.

Halfway to what used to be Mr. Tambor's saloon Danny heard his name called from somewhere down the street.

"Southern. Daniel Southern. Hold it right there, you little son of a bitch. You're under arrest!"

Danny spun around. He saw Brian Wright coming toward him. Brian had a badge on his coat and a pistol on his hip. Brian Wright for crying out loud! The kid who had been two grades behind Danny and his pals in school. Brian, who never had liked Danny anyway.

"Right there. You stay right there, damn you."

Danny looked left and right.

There was a sorrel horse — it looked like a good one — tied outside Meacham's Notions.

Brian was still coming.

Danny ran. Grabbed the reins from the post and vaulted into the saddle. He heeled the sorrel in the ribs and yanked its head around, away from Brian Wright.

"Hyah! Git, horse, git." The sorrel jumped into a run and tore belly-down through the middle of town.

Damn. Paley's Store. This was a day for memories, that was for sure. Danny tied the sorrel behind the building. He did not think he had been followed out of town — a town marshal's jurisdiction ended at the town limits, after all — but it never hurt to be careful. Especially since there seemed to be folks around who remembered musty old warrants. Dammit!

He walked around to the front and took a

look back toward town before he went inside.

"Hello. How can I help you?" It was Mr. Paley. Danny remembered him. He was kind of glad the old man was still alive.

"I was wondering, sir, does the stagecoach still stop here? The one connecting to the railroad?"

"Oh, yes. Every afternoon about three o'clock."

"What time would it be now, sir?"

Paley pulled a turnip-sized key-wind watch from his pocket and consulted it. " 'Bout one."

"Do I buy a ticket from you or from the driver?" Danny asked.

"Hugh will take your money. I just let him stop here to pick up or discharge passengers."

"Good. In that case, sir, I expect I'd like to buy something to eat. I haven't got around to that yet today."

"I can take care of that, all right," Paley said.

"Good. Thanks. I'll be right back."

Danny stepped outside and went around back. He removed the sorrel's bridle and tied it securely to the saddle strings, then gave the horse a slap on the butt to send it cantering away. Likely it would return home, wherever that was. He hoped so.

He did not even go through the saddlebags to see if there was anything in there that he wanted. He did not want anything that belonged to anyone else. Not anymore he didn't.

Danny turned and returned to Paley's Store, where the old man had pickled eggs and dried beef waiting for him along with some root beer to wash it down.

He did not know why, but all of a sudden he felt like crying.

14

Colorado 1886

He had been in a railroad station before. Of course he had. But that visit had been a little different. He and Red and Henry had thought about robbing the station at Garden City. All three of them went inside. He and Red looked the place over while Henry asked about tickets to some-dang-place.

There was probably a lot of money in a train station. Lots of passengers coming and going, and all of them laying out cash money for their tickets. Likely there was thousands in the till at a proper train station, but it was not a fit target for the three of them. There were too many people and too many guns. They looked that one station over and decided against trying it. The subject never came up again.

Now he would actually be getting on a train and riding in it. The prospect seemed more than a little worrisome.

Danny approached the railroad clerk's cage with trepidation. He cleared his throat twice before he could speak.

"I'd like a ticket, sir."

"All right." The clerk looked at him, the man's nose and eyes painted a ghoulish shade of green from the celluloid eyeshade he was wearing. He looked at Danny expectantly and waited. After a while he said, "Where to, son?"

"Oh, uh. Yeah." Danny could feel his cheeks turn warm. "I want to go . . . west. How far west do you go, sir?"

The clerk smiled a little. Probably he was a nice man. He did not poke fun at his customer's awkwardness. "This line goes to Pueblo, but you can transfer to another line if you want to go farther."

"All right then. I'll, uh, have one ticket to Pueblo." Danny paused, then realized his error. "Please."

"One to Pueblo. Yes, sir."

Danny had some time to kill so he walked down the street to Haversholm's and bought a Gladstone bag, two spare shirts, tooth powder and brush and socks. Before putting anything else into the bag, though, he unbuckled his gunbelt, carefully wrapped the belt ends around his holster and put that into the bag.

The rest of his new things he folded and put in with the revolver.

With any kind of luck, he was done with guns now. At least so far as his old trade was concerned. He might like to take up hunting someday. Perhaps for quail or prairie chickens if he could learn to use a shotgun. But no more robbing. Never. He swore it.

The train ride was a disappointment. He had been frightened of the speed, frightened at the thought of going so fast. But as it turned out, there really was no discomfort, no sense of rushing doom that he had anticipated.

The train swayed and bumped some, but less than a stagecoach or wagon, and he certainly was comfortable traveling in those.

What he had not expected was the stink of it.

Coal smoke and cinders blew in the open windows. The smoke was a heavy, slightly nauseating smell, while the cinders were frequently live and would leave a burn mark wherever they touched. It was no wonder so many travelers wore dusters over their clothing.

Still, the train travel was as swift and effortless as everyone said. Danny quickly adjusted to it. More or less. He doubted he would ever become so casual about train travel that he would be able to close his eyes and nap the way so many of his fellow passengers did.

He had a hollow, empty feeling as he fled west. He was leaving behind everything and everyone he had ever known. He hoped.

In Pueblo, Danny and a host of other passengers crowded into cabs for the transfer across town to the Denver & Rio Grande terminal. Once there, Danny joined the queue waiting for a ticket agent.

"Yes, sir. Where to?"

"How far west do you go?"

"Leadville."

"I've heard of it. Is it nice?"

"It's rich, and there's work to be had there. Is that what you'd call nice?"

Danny smiled. "Yes, sir, I expect that it is. I'll take a ticket to Leadville, please."

"One way, I assume?"

"Yes, sir. One way."

The man started tearing ticket forms and bashing them with a rather odd stamping device. Danny waited patiently. He was in no hurry now.

■ ■ ■ ■

The rails followed the Arkansas River, twisting through deep gorges where the world was in shadow, winding past steep, gray, barren walls of rock, hillsides of rock, meadows surrounded by rock. Danny was distinctly uncomfortable. He had never seen the mountains before. Not up close. He had barely come close enough before to see them on the horizon, lying like permanent clouds with their white caps.

He hated the gray lifelessness that he saw on both sides of the railroad. He was cold too. The farther the road climbed into the mountains, the lower the temperature.

"Is it always this cold?" he asked a mining engineer who had the seat across from his.

"This cold? Boy, you haven't seen cold yet. In Leadville this would be a hot summer day. I've seen it snow there in August."

"You're serious?"

"Damn right, I am."

Danny had no coat. But then he had not thought he would need one.

He was cold, he was miserable and he did not like these ugly mountains.

Majestic, some said. Beautiful? Bah! They were frightening, and he did not want to live in them.

"Excuse me. Do you know if there is a way to get over to the other side of these mountains?"

"West, you mean?" The gentleman shrugged. "Sure, I suppose you could do that. There's a road. Not a railroad but a regular road. You could get off up here at Buena Vista and take a stagecoach over to the west slope. All the way to Utah if you're of a mind to go that far."

"Buena Vista, you said."

The fellow nodded. "It's the second stop up the line from here."

"Thank you, sir. I think maybe I'll do that."

Danny looked out the train windows at the bleak, empty masses of gray rock and shivered. Kansas and the Nations had never been like this.

He felt better, though, at the prospect of getting out of these mountains just as quickly as he could.

The stage line ticket agent looked up from his papers and smiled. "Can I help you?"

"Yes, sir, I . . . Just a second." Danny dug in his pockets. He had not realized how lavishly he had been spending. On clothing and food and mostly on transportation tickets for one conveyance or another. He had very little money left.

He laid it all down, all but one dollar that he saved for food when he got to wherever it was he was going.

"How far will this take me?"

15

Western Colorado 1889

"Good morning, Danny."

"Good morning, sir." Danny looked up from his papers to see Anse Newhouse hang his hat on the elk-horn rack, on a tine above Danny's, remove his coat and hang it as well, then slip on a pair of elastic sleeve garters.

Newhouse was the station manager for Tomlinson & Dale Express, which ran both passenger coaches and freight in and out of the valley. Danny had recently been appointed as assistant manager. That increase in salary should make it possible now for him to formally propose marriage to Claire Hightower. Finally. It was something half the people in the valley knew was coming. That fact did not make Danny any the less nervous about her answer.

"Did you take the stock report from Liam?" Newhouse asked.

"Yes, sir. The gray's foot is still sore. He wants to hold it out of service a little longer while it heals." Liam Talen was in charge of the barn, including all rolling stock and draft horses. Danny handled the procurement of feed, payment of any obligations and general office work.

"He thinks it should heal all right. He packed the hoof with grease and fitted a felt pad under the shoe. Another three or four days should do it, Liam said."

"No problems otherwise?" Newhouse asked.

"No, sir, everything is fine."

The boss grinned, causing the tips of his mustache to rise and wiggle. "There's a picnic at the Methodist Church come Sunday."

"Oh, really?" Danny feigned surprise.

"Do you think you might be interested?"

"Possibly." It was his hope to slip away from the crowd and take Claire down by the creek. That would be a nice place to put forward his proposal, he thought.

"If you don't have anything better to do that day?"

"If I don't," Danny agreed.

Newhouse looked at Danny, who was struggling to maintain a straight face. Then both of them burst out laughing.

No, it was no secret at all what Danny intended, and apparently the whole town had figured out when as well.

He just hoped he did not have an audience, half the community gathered in a semicircle amid the trees come Sunday, to watch Daniel Southern get down on a knee and ask the girl to marry him.

"Good afternoon, Reverend. Something I can help you with?"

"Actually, Daniel, I was wondering if there was anything *I* could help *you* with." The preacher smiled.

"Oh, uh . . . we'll see." Danny shrugged and grinned. "Talk to me about it next week."

"I see. Going to ask her at the picnic next Sunday, are you?"

"Now, I didn't say that, Reverend. Not exactly."

The pastor's smile grew wider. "Close enough, Daniel. Close enough. I will put you down for counseling on Monday evening, if you like."

"Whatever you think, Reverend. If, uh, if there is a need."

The gentleman touched the brim of his hat and, silently chuckling, left the freight office.

■ ■ ■ ■

"Danny, could you do me a favor, please?"

"Sure, Anse. What d'you need?"

"I'm still knee-deep in these monthly reports, and they have to go out on tonight's eastbound or the home office will flay me alive."

Danny laughed. Anse Newhouse's battles with the obligatory reports were legendary. At least inside the company, they were. The man just hated them and because of that fussed over them trying to make them perfect. It would have been simpler for him to tell Danny to do it. Or to do it himself day by day. Instead he insisted on waiting until the last moment and then getting in a dither over them. "How can I help you, boss?"

Newhouse pointed to a small, brown canvas bag lying on his desk. "Could you take these receipts over to the bank for me, please? They close in twenty minutes and there is no way on God's green earth that I'll be done in time to take them."

"I'll be glad to, Anse."

"You're a lifesaver, Danny. Thanks."

Danny removed the green celluloid eye-shade he customarily wore when he was at his desk. He stood and stretched, yawning, then stepped over to Newhouse's desk and reached for the deposit bag. "I'll be back in ten minutes."

Newhouse grinned. "Unless Claire is there. In which case I won't get another lick of work out of you today."

Danny laughed. But he did not dispute what Anse said. Claire did indeed sometimes drop by the bank, where her father was head teller. And if he should happen to run into her this afternoon . . .

Danny reached for the doorknob at the same instant a large man in a rumpled, badly fitted suit came out of the bank. The man wore a revolver — rare around here — and a scowl. "Get outa my way, you."

Instead of waiting for Danny to step aside, the fellow barged straight ahead, deliberately shouldering Danny out of his way and striding away down the street. Danny stood for a moment watching him, half-tempted to go call the son of a bitch for the insult.

But Danny was not armed, and this stranger most certainly was.

Besides, the bastard was as big as a brood sow. And about as courteous as a boar hog. Better to leave things be.

Danny stood there for a few moments

longer to let his hackles lie down. Then he fashioned a smile on his face.

The smile became genuine as soon as he stepped inside and saw Claire perched on a stool behind the counter.

All thoughts of the man outside were forgotten.

"I, uh, I was thinking, I could . . . after supper, that is . . . along toward the cool of the evening . . . I was thinking I could call at your house and we, uh, we could maybe go for a walk? Down along the creek, I mean. Just for, uh, a little while."

Claire reached out and took his hand. Just for a moment. Down behind the side of the counter, where people could not see except perhaps for her father. She gently pressed his fingers and then decorously stepped back, smiling.

"I wish I could," she said, "but we have choir practice tonight. I promised Pastor I would come. He wants me to do a duet with Jenny Field."

"I understand," Danny said.

And he did. Sort of. Understanding, however, is one thing; acceptance is another. He wished he could tell Claire to forget about choir and walk out with him. Probably she would do exactly that, too, except for her promise. Claire took very seriously the importance of a word once pledged.

"Maybe . . ." He smiled and shrugged. This was Monday. On Tuesdays Claire had the Literary Society. Wednesdays were evening prayer services. "Maybe Thursday," he said, saddened.

"Maybe Thursday," Claire whispered in that sweet, soft voice he loved.

Very lightly Danny sought Claire's hand to squeeze when he said good-bye. What he wanted to do was to grab her, kiss her, put his tongue so far down her throat that she gagged. His expression, however, showed nothing but polite interest.

Disappointed, he transferred his attention to Mr. Hightower and the express company's deposit.

Anse Newhouse sat back in his swivel chair and laced his fingers behind his neck. The man was smiling, and the cap was on the ink pot.

"Good night, sir," Danny said, chuckling to himself.

"Good night, Danny." Newhouse would stay and see the evening stage off . . . with the monthly reports aboard.

The sun was almost to the horizon, but the light in the sky had not yet begun to fade. It was too early for supper. And there was no hope of seeing Claire tonight. What he needed, Danny decided, was a game of billiards. And a beer. Maybe a beer and a shot to go with it. He was feeling at loose ends this evening, although he did not know why. The disappointment of not being able to spoon and cuddle with Claire perhaps.

Instead of turning toward his rooming house, Danny went in the other direction, toward the Sailor's Rest, where Andrew Garza claimed to have once been a seafaring man but now owned a quiet saloon where a man might find a tipple but not a fight. There were other watering holes available to those who preferred a little rowdiness with their fun. Oddly, the reputation of sailors aside, Garza did not allow any whores in his place, which quite possibly explained why there was so little trouble at the Sailor's Rest.

Danny happened to know, because he was in charge of having it hauled in, that all of the saloons brought their beer in from the same supplier, and all of them charged the same amount for a drink. The differences were in the surroundings, not the products.

There had been a time in his life when he might have chosen a livelier establishment, but now the Sailor's Rest suited him just fine.

He stepped inside the batwings and paused for a moment for his eyes to adjust to the relative darkness.

The first thing he saw was the big man who had been coming out of the bank. The fellow had a glass mug in his hand and his foot propped on the brass rail. He was talking to two gents who were wearing linen dusters and slouch hats.

Danny went to the bar and reached for a pickled sausage on the free lunch plate. "Draw me a beer will you please, Andrew."

"One beer. Coming right up."

The sausage was good, the flavor clean and vinegary. He leaned forward to get some soda crackers to go with it.

"Jesus God!" a voice to the right of the big fellow blurted. "I thought you was dead."

"Red? Henry? Good Lord!" Danny rushed around the big man and grabbed his two old friends, hugging both of them, all three trying to speak at once.

"Danny, this is our partner George Mc-Colm. He, um, you know it takes three to properly do things the way we do. After you was killed . . . ," he laughed, sounding more than a little nervous about it, "after we *thought* you was killed, we figured we'd best be gone from that country for a spell. We hooked up with George in Denver. He'd been trying to rob the mails by himself, but he saw that our way was better. Less shooting, and that means less interest in pursuit. They don't chase as hard when the only harm is to some insurance company back East." Red grinned. "But why am I telling you all this? You already know it as good as I do. Hell, a lot of it was your ideas t' begin with."

"Where the devil have you boys been?" Danny asked. "I haven't heard a thing about you in all these years."

"Up north," Henry put in. "Montana, Idaho, the Dakotas some."

"We got to Canada too, if you can believe it. Mighty good pickings up there."

"For a while. Lately things've been getting kinda hot." Henry shrugged. "So we come down here for a change of scenery."

"Damn, it's good t' see you, Danny. So tell us about yourself." Red lowered his voice. "What're you here to hit?"

"Boys," Danny said, "I'm not 'hitting' anything. I've gone straight. I live here. I'm clean. Have been for years. Why, I haven't even strapped on a gun for I can't remember how long. Nor had any need to."

When he mentioned what he was doing for a living, Red's eyes lit and McColm took an interest in the conversation for the first time.

"You're in charge of the freight? Jesus, Danny, that's perfect." His voice dropped to a whisper again. "We come here to do the bank, but this could be even better. We can find a place somewheres not too far. You can spot the targets for us, and we'll bring you in for a full share of whatever we get. Why, this could be way the hell better than one shot at the bank. With you checking all the cargoes we'd have a steady flow of all the work we could ever want. Pick off the plums as we want them an' let life go by. Damn, but this is perfect."

Danny shook his head. "I'm sorry, boys, but I can't do that. I have a good life here. I like these folks. I'm even thinking of getting married. Gonna pop the question to her on Sunday. It will be a few months before the actual wedding, but I'd sure be honored if you boys showed up to stand with me." He frowned in deep thought. "Can a fella have two best men, both at the same time I wonder? I'd sure like that if the preacher would go along with it. Imagine! All three of us together, and the two of you as my best men. It couldn't get any better than that."

McColm turned to face the three. "Look, you assholes can plan a tea party if you like, but I'm telling you, we came here to hit something and we damn sure will. If you don't want to tip us to the mail pouches, Southern, then we'll do the bank, just like we planned to begin with."

"No, you won't," Danny said, his jaw set to a stubborn angle.

"Why the hell not?"

"My girlfriend's father works there, for one thing. For another, I know how much this community depends on that bank. It's important to them. They need it. They need what's in it. You can't go in there with guns and rob it."

McColm glared at Danny in silence for a moment, then turned his attention to Red and Henry. "Tell him to grow up, will you. And tell him to stay the hell out of my way because we are going to take that bank and there is not one damn thing he can do about it. Now you three children jabber at one another all you like. Me, I'm gonna go have something to eat and figure out the best way for us to ride out of here with our saddle-bags full."

McColm again bumped Danny with a

shoulder as he bulled his way past.

"I guess . . . Look, Danny, you don't have t' actually *do* anything. We won't even ask you no questions, so there won't be anything you got to feel bad about afterward. But if George says we're gonna do it, then, well, I guess we are."

"Red, I can't believe you're saying this. The man you want to rob is my future father-in-law. He's a good man. He doesn't deserve this shit."

"We're gonna take the bank, Danny. I'm sorry, but that's just the way it is."

"D'you mean to tell me that you took Mc-Colm into your gang and showed him the ropes and now he thinks he's running the show?"

"But Danny," Henry said softly, "George *is* running things."

"I don't understand that. How could . . . ?"

"Him and Red fought over it, Danny. You know me. I don't much care about such things. But Red . . . they fought."

Red had been looking away while Henry said that. As if by not seeing his friend's expression he could pretend he did not hear the hurtful words.

"Well, hell," Danny said, "of course a big

bastard like that could whip Red. The guy looks to be all muscle."

"It wasn't fists they fought with, Danny. It was a gunfight. Sort of a gunfight anyway. George had his pistol out an' cocked an' ready to fire before Red ever got his out of the leather. He said for Red to back down or die. He's been the head of the gang ever since."

"Then why the devil do you stay with him? Why ride with someone that'd do that to one of you?"

"Jeez, Danny, we need for there to be three of us and . . . well . . . you know."

Danny did not know. Not about that. What he did know was "Fellas, I never thought I'd have to say any such of a thing, but comes the time you try and take this bank here, I'll stand against you."

"Against three of us?"

"You can't do that, Danny. You can't."

"Hell, you don't even wear a gun."

"And you weren't much good with one when you did carry one every day."

"Leave it be, Danny. Leave it be."

Danny sighed. "I have to stand against you on this, boys. It's the right thing to do."

"Do folks around here know about you, Danny? Do they know about your past? You was as bad as us once. Do they know that?"

"No, they don't."

"Then you prob'ly should keep your mouth shut. If I ever have to look at things through jail cell bars, Danny, I'll tell enough to put you in with us."

Danny smiled. "I've been in worse company," he said.

He put his hands on their shoulders, on both Red and Henry, and he squeezed. "Excuse me now, boys. I think I need t' go home and do some thinking."

"Remember what I said, Danny. If you stand against us, you'll either be shot down by George McColm or you'll wind up in jail for what the three of us done back in Kansas an' the Nations. And you know I don't lie."

"I know that, Red. You may stretch hell out o' the truth, but you're no liar. Now, excuse me, please. I want to go home now."

16

Danny glanced at the lemonade on the tray. The ice had long since melted, and it must have been an hour past that Yvonne slipped into the room to light the lamps and then scamper out again. Claire had hardly moved in all that time.

"Is this why you told Mr. Newhouse you were sick and couldn't work?"

He nodded. "I've been . . . fretting. Trying to work out the best thing to do. Now I know. I'll stop them from going inside, Claire. I owe you that. Your father could be hurt. This whole town would be hurt. I can't allow any of that. But before . . . before I stand against them, honey, I wanted you to know. Everything. I reckon . . . now you do."

"May I ask you something?"

"Anything. I'll not lie to you, whatever it is."

"That girl," she began, then faltered.

Danny's brows knitted. "That girl? What

girl do you mean?"

"Back in the Indian Nations. The Kiowa I believe you said she was."

"Oh, yeah. What about her?"

"You lived with her. Did you love her?"

Danny shook his head. "She was a good girl. I liked her and her son, both o' them. But I never loved anybody till I met you, Claire. An' I never will again."

Claire nodded and sat back in her chair.

After a moment Danny said, "That's it? I tell you all about a life of crime, robbing folks and raising hel— Cain . . . and all you ask me about is some Indian girl that kept house for me a long time ago?"

"She did more than just keep house, didn't she?" Claire asked primly.

"Yeah. Yeah, she did. But I said I'd tell you all the truth. I reckon that was part of it."

"All right then. That subject is closed. Danny, what are you going to do?"

"First thing, I'd sure like to know where you stand. If you want me out of your life now. If you hate me now that you know the truth about me."

"Danny, I love you. Don't you know that?"

"I've hoped that you do. Hoped this day would never come too, but here it is. D'you still want me, Claire honey?"

"I will always want you, Danny. I will be honored to be your wife."

Danny turned pale. "Good Lord. I guess I've gone and proposed, haven't I?"

She laughed, her laughter the sound of delicate bells in his heart. "Yes, and in case you missed it, dear, I accepted."

Claire became serious. After a moment her eyes began to well with tears. "Danny, I just realized. You . . . you don't expect to live when you face this McColm person. Do you?"

"Do me a favor, honey?"

"Anything, Danny, even . . . you know."

He shook his head vigorously. "No. I'll not do anything to harm you, Claire. What I want . . . Would you pray for me? Please?"

She rushed to him. Dropped to her knees before him and hugged him tight, as if she never wanted to let go. She cried silently.

"Why are you sitting over there, Danny?"

"I just . . . Do you mind?"

"No, I don't mind," Newhouse said. "It's just not where you normally sit."

Danny did not really want to explain that from here he could see the front of the bank. From here he could see if the boys showed up to rob it. *When* they showed up, that is.

"I have the livestock report ready whenever you want to go over it," he said.

Danny grabbed his hat off the rack and hurried out, lifting the safety thong off the hammer of his Colt and shoving it out of the way. The boys were riding in, the three of them close together on horses that had wide chests and gleaming coats. McColm was in the lead, with Red and Henry flanking him on either side.

Danny broke into a trot and then a run. He reached the sidewalk in front of the bank before they did.

"Well, lookit what we have here," McColm said, sneering. "You weren't wearing a gun the last time we seen you, Southern. Be careful with it. A boy could hurt himself with one of them things."

McColm swung down off his saddle. Red and Henry did also. Henry reached over and took the reins of all three horses, then stepped backward a foot or so. Danny got the idea that Henry did not want any part of this. Good. That meant he only had two to contend with, either of them faster with a gun than he'd been to begin with. And he had not so much as touched a revolver since he left Pueblo all those years ago.

"You're standing in our way, boy," Mc-

Colm said.

"Yes, I am." He made no threats. It would have been pointless to bother trying. He simply stood there.

"Move aside, Southern."

Danny's heart was pounding. He felt light-headed and just a little bit woozy, a little bit detached from this that was happening.

"I said *move!*"

Danny said nothing. He stood motionless. Determined not to move no matter what. Literally *no matter what.*

"Step outa the way, boy, or draw that shooter. Do it *now.*"

Danny reached for the hard, polished walnut grips of his revolver. He made no attempt to get his gun out faster than George McColm. He knew he could not. His only chance to stop them, he believed, was with sheer determination. He might be slow, but with luck he could get his shot off before he went down.

McColm was unbelievably fast. His gun was in hand before Danny had time to begin his draw.

Danny saw the halo of flame that enveloped the muzzle of McColm's pistol. He felt the concussion of the tightly focused explosion.

The shot was fast but not aimed. Danny

heard glass breaking behind him.

He got his fingers wrapped around the grips of his Colt.

McColm fired again. Danny felt a blow low on his left hip. It was not as bad as he'd feared; it was no harder than Red used to hit when they were boys and sometimes fought. It was enough to turn him partially around.

He pulled his gun free of the leather, dragging the hammer back before it ever came clear.

Noise. Make enough noise. Get the eyes of the town on them. It would not be possible for them to go inside the bank to rob it. There would not be time enough for them to do that.

McColm fired a third shot. Danny felt the burn of superheated lead slicing across his flesh just below his ribs.

His Colt came level. His knees were weak and he was sagging down toward the sidewalk.

But he got his shot off. His one shot.

It took George McColm in the gut, doubling him over. His revolver fell into the dirt of the small-town street and he toppled over on top of it.

Danny was on his knees, gun still in hand although he did not seem to have strength enough to lift it.

Not that he wanted to lift it.

Red and Henry were already vaulting into their saddles, ready to make a run for safety.

"Boys," Danny said, "I don't think I oughta invite you two back for the wedding."

"We'll send a present," Red said.

Henry grinned. "A peck of fresh oysters packed in ice."

"I sure wish you could be with me."

None of them paid any attention to McColm, who was gasping for air and turning blue.

"Get outa here, boys. Hurry."

Red and Henry wheeled their horses away and put the spurs to them. Danny tried to watch them out of town, but somewhere along there his vision clouded.

The next thing he knew Claire was beside him. His head was in her lap, and she was crying.

"Dammit, woman," he whispered, "are you gonna cry the whole time we're married?"

"Will you please be quiet. The doctor is coming."

"Yes, ma'am." He blacked out again, but he was content. No matter what came now, he was content.

We hope you have enjoyed this Large Print book. Other Thorndike, Wheeler, and Chivers Press Large Print books are available at your library or directly from the publishers.

For information about current and upcoming titles, please call or write, without obligation, to:

Publisher
Thorndike Press
295 Kennedy Memorial Drive
Waterville, ME 04901
Tel. (800) 223-1244

or visit our Web site at:

http://gale.cengage.com/thorndike

OR

Chivers Large Print
published by BBC Audiobooks Ltd
St James House, The Square
Lower Bristol Road
Bath BA2 3SB
England
Tel. +44(0) 800 136919
email: bbcaudiobooks@bbc.co.uk
www.bbcaudiobooks.co.uk

All our Large Print titles are designed for easy reading, and all our books are made to last.